IRON HEART

SLATER SIBLINGS SERIES #3

MISSY WALKER

For you, dear reader, who has pressed pause and taken a moment out of this chaotic world for yourself.

I

KINGSLEY

T-minus three hours until I'm on a plane to Australia. My New York apartment, with its panoramic views of the city, offers a solitude that is both comforting and imposing. Everything here is controlled, precise, just how I like it.

Lola, my submissive for the evening, kneels before me. Her eyes are lowered, and she is still, waiting for a command, a sign of what I want from her. But I'm already distancing myself, my mind shifting to the responsibilities that await me overseas.

"Is there anything else you require, Master?" she asks, breaking the silence, her voice soft and respectful.

I consider her question, my mind already cataloging the tasks that need to be accomplished before my departure—meetings to schedule, reports to review, a whole world of control that never stops demanding.

"No," I reply, my voice measured and unemotional as ever. "You've done well."

She bows her head. "Thank you, Master."

I rise, moving to the window. The city stretches out before me, a chaotic dance of lights and shadows, full of life and yet somehow empty.

Like me.

Lola doesn't move, doesn't speak. She's been well-trained, understanding the boundaries and the rules, just like all the others from the agency I use.

Time is slipping away, and I can't afford to linger. There are people relying on me, and I won't let them down. My life is a carefully constructed machine, and I'm the one holding the controls.

"I'll make arrangements for your transportation home," I tell her, my back still to her.

Her acknowledgment is a soft, "Yes, Master."

I head to my study, checking my email and reviewing my itinerary. Everything is in order, meticulously planned and executed. Just like always.

Back in the living room, Lola has not moved. A pang of something unexpected hits me when I look at her. A fleeting connection? No, that's impossible. I don't allow connections.

"You may leave," I tell her, and she rises, her movements graceful and controlled.

"Safe travels, Master," she says, and there's a longing in her voice I refuse to acknowledge.

The car is waiting when I leave the apartment, and I sink into the back seat, allowing the familiar streets of New York to pass me by in a blur.

With practiced efficiency, I arrive at the airport, moving through security, and board the plane. Settling into my seat, I pull out my laptop, already focused on the work that awaits me.

The plane takes off, the city falling away beneath me, and I feel a strange sense of loss. Not for Lola, not for the fleeting pleasure she provided, but for something deeper, something I can't quite identify.

But it's gone in an instant, replaced by the cool, calculating focus that has become my shield.

Control, precision, detachment.

Principles I have lived by ever since leaving school and joining the 75th Ranger Regiment in the US Army.

As the plane cruises toward Australia, I immerse myself in my work, my world reduced to protecting a pop star.

I shake my head at what my life has been reduced to.

One year ago, Kingsley Williams, three times Silver Star recipient for gallantry fighting our enemy and risking one's own life in the call of duty.

Six months ago, I was honorably discharged.

"Mr. Williams?" a voice pulls me from my self-loathing. "Can I offer you a drink, sir?" the flight attendant smiles flirtatiously, and I forget I'm in first-class on someone else's dime.

"Whiskey, make it a double."

"Of course, sir," she says, staring at me like a love-sick puppy.

The sincerity in her look drags me back to the past. Carter, bleeding out, and his final words, *"Tell my wife I love her."* Three medals don't make up for the massacre on my team.

Fucking chunks of metal will never bring back my best friend or the other five men in my unit I lost that day. Anger builds inside me like a raging tornado.

I'm relieved when the attendant returns quickly, and I take the drink from her, downing it in one sitting. I meet her patronizing gaze head-on and hand her the empty glass. "One more, please," I request, and she grins and hurries away.

Another twenty-two hours until I touch down in Sydney. Plenty of time to get drunk, then sober up before my meeting.

2
VICTORIA

"At eight, you have three press calls, back-to-back, followed by interviews from various media outlets in the penthouse here. That should take you up to one, and then you have a brief thirty-minute window for lunch."

Lexy's words echo in my ears, but I'm still lost in the fog of exhaustion, remnants of applause from Sydney's entertainment precinct lingering in my mind. Four months on tour, and the exhaustion is no longer a sensation. It's a constant companion.

I take a slow, contemplative sip of green juice, an unfamiliar but supposedly healthy trend I'm trying to embrace, and force myself to focus on Lexy, my loyal assistant. She's rattling off the day's schedule, and I can't help but marvel at how this is considered a light day.

"Tomorrow," she continues, unfazed by my obvious distraction, "After your third show in Sydney, we have two more days of press and interviews, all lined up by the record company."

"Oh, I get to have lunch today?" I interject, my voice

dripping with sarcasm. Lexy offers a sly grin, clearly accustomed to my sarcasm.

"We have a soundcheck at two," Michael, my tour manager, adds, his eyes fixed on his tablet, orchestrating the whirlwind that is Viki Slate—a worldwide jazz-pop sensation. Or, as the *New York Post* recently called me, "the new Amy Winehouse" or *TMZ*'s viral article, "Jazz Pop Star's Journey from Ordeal to Stardom." A compliment but also a comparison that sends a chill down my spine.

Memories of the kidnapping rush back, and I can almost feel the kidnappers' hands on my body. Nausea stirs within me, an unwelcome reminder of what could have been my fate.

"Viki?" Lexy's concerned voice pulls me back to reality, and I look up to find both her and Michael studying me with worried eyes.

"I said your new bodyguard will be here at one," she repeats, concerned.

"For heaven's sake. Another one?" I groan, not bothering to hide my frustration.

"Well, you drove the others away," Lexy replies, her hand on her hip.

"They were all incompetent, dim-witted idiots!" I snap, and Michael lets out a strained chuckle, wisely choosing to stay out of our debate.

Lexy shoots him a warning glance before looking down at her clipboard, the symbol of her organized control over my chaotic life.

"His name is Kingsley," she says, pausing for effect. "Vincent hired him through an agency."

"My brother?" I raise an eyebrow, intrigued and a bit unsettled.

My family's involvement in my life is a double-edged

sword. I love my two brothers to a fault, but our strained relationship with our father continues to weigh on me, even if he's the one to blame for all this.

"Yes, both Julius and Vincent have vetted several agencies since the... *incident.* In the end, it was this particular bodyguard they wanted," Lexy explains, her voice softening.

"I see," I grumble, bitterness seeping into my words.

Lexy simply nods, understanding without judgment.

"What kind of name is Kingsley anyway?" I mutter, trying to lighten the mood.

"No idea." Lexy laughs. "But let's just hope you don't scare him away, huh?"

I roll my eyes, and Michael lets out another chuckle before excusing himself to take a call.

Lexy stays, though. She's become more than an assistant lately, more like a friend. Often, she's there when I can't bear to be alone, especially at night when fear threatens to overwhelm me. I never tell her the real reason, pretending it's all about the schedule. But somehow, I think she knows.

"And tell me about this new album of yours? What can we expect?"

I smile at the question. It's like they read it from a script. Other journalists have asked me the same question three times already this morning. But ever the performer, I smile and open my mouth to speak when a loud scuffle halts me. The sound originates from the suite's entrance area, and I lock eyes with the journalist, who also seems baffled, clearly picking up on the unusual noise. Immediately, my pulse quickens while my anxieties rush to the surface.

I rise to investigate, my throat choked by fear. Throwing open the door, I'm met with a scene of disarray—two of my existing security personnel are on the floor in a heated confrontation with a strikingly imposing man. His tall frame and stern expression make it clear he's not here to back down.

My assistant, Lexy, is beside herself, her face a mixture of exasperation and concern.

"What is this?" I snap, my eyes narrowing on the stranger.

He turns to me, his eyes cool and unapologetic, but something in his gaze catches me off guard. There's a defiance there, a fire I haven't seen in any of the other bodyguards I've had. And, to my surprise, I'm curious rather than scared.

"I'm Kingsley Williams, your new bodyguard," he states, his tone authoritative. "I found serious flaws in your security, and I was demonstrating them."

Is this guy for real?

"This is your idea of a demonstration?" I shoot back, my voice laced with skepticism. I take in the fallen men clutching at their torsos. "This is a circus! A complete lack of professionalism!"

Lexy interjects quickly, ushering the journalist toward the exit. "Thank you, Viki," he offers over his shoulder while Lexy leads him past the two security men, picking themselves off the floor with a whale of a groan. But I'm too annoyed to reply as I stare up at the hulk of a man in front of me.

"I call it necessary," he shoots back, his jaw set. "Your safety is my priority, and I won't pretend everything's fine when it's not. This..." he motions to the guards, "... is a goddamn joke."

I stare at him, torn between anger at his audacity and a reluctant admiration for his boldness. He's unlike anyone I've encountered before, and I can't quite decide how I feel about that.

He's a giant, cloaked in all black, looking like a lethal weapon made of muscles and broad shoulders. Dark brown eyes and slick hair with his olive complexion give him an air of dangerous charm. He speaks with a rugged American accent, and when he turns to face the security he so easily tossed to the floor, I catch a glimpse of a tattoo on his neck just above his collar. That symbol just adds another layer to his whole mysterious vibe.

Everything about him screams authority, but his unapologetic approach and clear conviction in his mission irritate and attract me. The way he's challenged my security —and, by extension, me—ignites a fire in my belly. I'm used to being in control, but something tells me this man won't be easily swayed or manipulated.

Our eyes lock again, and the intensity of his gaze sends a shiver down my spine. There's a challenge in those eyes, a promise of uncompromising protection mixed with a stubborn will that matches my own.

"I don't need a rogue playing games with my security," I growl out, my frustration mounting. "I need someone who respects protocol."

"Protocol that fails you?" he challenges, his voice low and intense. "I'm here to protect you, not coddle your ego."

My face flushes with anger, but a part of me recognizes the truth in his words. "And who are you to decide what I need?" I snap, my voice trembling with emotion.

"Someone who takes his job seriously," he replies, his

eyes locked on mine. "Someone who won't lie to you or sugarcoat the truth."

We stand there, our gazes locked in a battle of wills, the tension in the air thick and palpable. A strange sensation twists in my gut. I'm both furious and fascinated by this man.

Finally, I break the silence, my voice tight with barely contained anger. "Fine. But know this... I won't tolerate any more stunts like this."

He meets my challenge head-on. "No stunts required... *if* security is sorted."

"I'll take that lunch now, Lexy," I snap when Lexy returns.

"And your meeting with Kingsley?" she asks sheepishly, side-glancing him, then me.

I narrow my eyes and take him in.

"I think we've had enough introductions for one day. You can take me to my sound check tomorrow."

"Affirmative," he replies with a curt nod that only annoys me further.

My hands tremble with fury when I retreat to my hotel room, my mind replaying the audacity of Kingsley's actions. The way he handled my security team, his smug confidence, and his disarming presence leaves me reeling and deeply unsettled.

My lunch is a salad, though all I crave is a messy cheeseburger and fries. Something about comfort food feels appropriate now, but I can't eat. I need to vent, and there's only one person who will understand.

I dial Vincent's number, and my brother picks up on the second ring. "Vincent, what the hell have you done?" I explode, unable to contain my anger.

"What's wrong, Victoria?" Vincent's voice is calm, with a hint of concern.

"That new bodyguard of yours, *Kingsley,* just caused a scene outside my interview room! He tossed my security detail around like they were toys!" My words tumble out, fueled by frustration and disbelief.

"Slow down, slow down," Vincent says, trying to soothe me. "I knew Kingsley was going to evaluate the security, but I didn't think he'd go to such lengths. Let me explain—"

"Explain? Vincent, he made a spectacle of himself and me!" I snap, pacing the floor.

"Victoria, hear me out," Vincent implores, his voice firm yet gentle. "Kingsley is ex-Special Forces. He was leader of the 3rd Regiment Battalion."

"I don't even know what that means," I snap back.

"Listen. He's the best there is. He is the recipient of three Silver Stars, and he's the only bodyguard qualified enough who would take the job after you fired everyone else. You have a reputation now. You're lucky to have him. They don't come any more highly decorated than him."

I stop, Vincent's words sinking in. Despite my anger, I hate that he's right. I need someone like Kingsley—someone who's different and has the guts to challenge and keep me safe.

"He could have handled this privately, Vincent," I say, my voice cracking. "He didn't have to embarrass me like that."

"Give him a chance," Vincent urges. "I know it's hard to trust after what happened, but he's there to protect you. He's the best, and he takes his job very seriously."

I let out a long, shaky breath, my emotions in turmoil. Vincent's words make sense, but Kingsley's actions have rattled me. Still, something about him intrigues me, even as it infuriates me.

"I'll try," I finally say, a mixture of resignation and curiosity in my voice. "But if he pulls another stunt like that, he's gone."

Vincent lets out a groan. "We only want what's best for you, sis. I have to run. Take care... I love you."

"I love you too," I reply, ending the call.

I sink into a chair, my eyes on the untouched salad. *Kingsley.* The name lingers, and I can't shake the image of him—his unflinching gaze, his cold, powerful presence.

He's not like the others.

He's something else entirely.

3

KINGSLEY

We're already behind schedule.

Her tardiness and attitude are something I simply cannot tolerate.

I'm beginning to question my decision to take on this assignment.

Since being honorably discharged from the Special Forces six months ago, my former Sergeant Stanley has called me weekly. Drinking myself further into a hole and blaming myself for losing my team, Stanley put forward my name to his brother, who happened to be on the lookout for a uniquely trained person to guard a new client.

His brother runs a top-tier security firm specializing in VIPs and needed a highly trained bodyguard to protect Victoria Slater or Viki Slate, her stage name.

The last thing I wanted was a gig in bodyguarding some rich pop star. But the alternative? Suicide was too easy. I couldn't do that. So I took the gig.

During the preparation, I delved deep into her past, looking up her former residences, current details, and her recent kidnapping in Asia. It had taken up space in my mind that was previously occupied with negativity and self-loathing.

As I simmer with anger, the room around me grows frigid while I await her to come out of her hotel room. My attention briefly shifts when my phone buzzes, and when I glance at the screen, I see a message from my sister, Indy.

Indy: *How's the assignment?*

I quickly thumb out a reply, knowing I'll be busy but will make sure to call her later.

Me: *This woman is intolerable.*

I slide my phone back into my pocket and look up, I find her assistant, Lexy, giving me a comforting smile. "She's often a bit late," Lexy concedes.

The poor woman appears worn out and stressed, no doubt from the challenges of managing a celebrity's demanding schedule.

But now that I'm on the job, I'm appalled at the way things were handled before. It seems her security was composed of mere amateurs, all employed by the record label, providing the same level of protection they offer their entire roster of stars. But her fame has risen to new heights, and therefore, the level of security must adapt to threats abound.

My anger bubbles over. "If she wants protection, then we need to adhere to a strict schedule, a timeline where I know her whereabouts at all times. I can't protect someone who can't keep to a schedule."

My patience at an end, I knock sharply on her door, ignoring Lexy's soft growl of disapproval.

"Ms. Slater," I call out, repeating myself for the second time.

The car and her security detail are ready and waiting downstairs.

"Jesus, 'I'm coming!" she yells back, her voice tinged with irritation.

With a swift motion, she opens the door, and the fragrance of her perfume reaches me. She's petite, no more than five feet five inches with striking auburn hair and intense blue eyes that seem ready to shoot daggers at me. Casually dressed in black leggings and a bright red high-neck top, she's a perplexing mixture of enchanting beauty and infuriating annoyance.

"Seriously, move out of my way," she snaps.

Good. She should hate me.

"We are late," I remind her coolly.

"I'm the one who sets the time around here," she replies, puffing herself up and brushing past me.

I dismiss her comment and follow her down the elevators. As we pile out, I direct the rest of the security team to follow us in the other car while we make our way to the stadium venue.

Lexy, Victoria, and I pile into the black Suburban, the tension still palpable as we pull away from the hotel. The drive will take approximately twenty-eight minutes, and I intend to use that time to ensure our plans are synchronized.

Victoria's piercing blue eyes flicker toward me, filled with a mixture of annoyance and curiosity. "So what's the big plan, then?" she asks, her voice laced with sarcasm.

I keep my gaze fixed on the road, not allowing myself to be drawn into an unnecessary battle of wills. "We're going to stick to a schedule," I say firmly. "One that ensures your safety and allows you to focus on what you do best."

Lexy watches the exchange, a hint of amusement in her eyes. She knows her boss well and seems to take my unwavering approach in stride.

Victoria snorts, crossing her arms. "I've managed fine without being micromanaged. Why change things now?"

"Because," I respond calmly. "Your previous security was ill-equipped to handle your level of fame and the risks that come with it. I'm here to make sure nothing compromises your well-being."

She looks like she wants to argue further, but instead, she turns her gaze to the window, watching the cityscape rush by.

The ride continues in relative silence, the thrum of the engine and the occasional chatter on the security radio filling the space. Lexy takes the opportunity to go over some last-minute details with her, and I'm surprised by the relentless demands on this woman.

As we approach the stadium, the magnitude of the venue and the event becomes clear. Fans are already gathering, a sea of eager faces and waving banners. Security personnel are visible at strategic points, and the entire operation seems to be a well-orchestrated symphony of anticipation. But even from this far, I can see holes in the security.

"We're here," I announce, pulling into the secured area reserved for the performers and their teams.

Victoria's eyes sparkle with a renewed energy. "Let's make it a night to remember," she says, her voice now filled with determination rather than annoyance.

I allow myself a small smile, appreciating her spirit. "That's the plan, Ms. Slater."

As we approach the VIP entrance of the stadium, a group of rogue fans who've managed to slip into this restricted area catches my eye. Their excitement is palpable when they recognize the vehicle.

Victoria spots them too, her face lighting up with a

warm smile as they rush forward. She waves at them through the tinted windows, clearly wanting to acknowledge their enthusiasm.

"Stay in the car," I instruct, my voice firm while I assess the situation.

"They're just fans, and they love me," she argues, still waving. "They won't do anything."

"This area is off-limits," I reply, reaching for the door handle.

Before I can stop her, Victoria opens her door and steps out, her face determined. "They deserve my time," she says, moving toward the fans.

My heart jumps into my throat when I follow her, my protective instincts on high alert. "Miss Slater, please get back in the car," I call out, but she ignores me.

One particularly eager fan approaches her, his eyes wide with admiration. I move to intervene and push him back, but Victoria beats me to it, extending her hand to him and apologizing. "I'm so sorry about my new security," she says, giving me a sharp look. "They're still getting used to how I do things."

I sense my nostrils widening while she continues to autograph items for fans. The irritation she feels toward me is clearly reciprocated on my end.

I stand by, my body tense, watching her interact with the fans, aware I've overstepped a boundary in her eyes. My job is to protect her, but I've also crossed a line in her world where connecting with her fans is paramount.

As stadium security finally arrives to disperse the fans, Victoria turns her eyes, shooting daggers at me. "Don't ever treat my fans like that again," she says, her voice low and cold.

"My job is to protect you," I reply, my voice equally firm.

"I don't need protection from the people who love me," she replies, her face set in a stubborn expression.

She glides by me, and while her perfume would normally be inviting, her foul mood taints its sweetness as she makes her way to the stadium. The tension between us hangs heavy in the air.

Within fifteen minutes, she's on stage for the sound check. I've already met with Michael, her tour manager, and reviewed the on-site schematics. Everything appears to be in order.

While she's engaged with that, I'm busy analyzing the VIP area, stage, and green room, looking for any vulnerabilities where an ambush might occur.

I find myself watching her on stage, captivated by her presence. Victoria greets her full band with an enthusiasm and energy that catch me off guard. A total contrast of how she is with me.

She seems to come alive once the music starts and she grabs the microphone. I'm not familiar with her music, but there's no denying the soulful quality of her voice. She starts with a slow ballad. It's a sexy, jazzy vibe, and I see a side of her that genuinely intrigues me.

A sudden warmth trails down my spine, a sensation that hits me in a place I'm not expecting. I suppress the feeling, recognizing that I'm wound too tightly around her, like I could snap.

"Right, that's a wrap," she announces after an hour, thanking her band, stepping off the stage where I'm waiting.

"Outstanding performance! You nailed it!" Michael says, stepping out from the production desk area at the side of the stage.

"Freaking phenomenal!" Lexy adds, beaming.

"I know, right? The sound, the stage. I can't wait till showtime," Victoria replies, excitement in her voice. She removes her inner ear monitors and pauses, standing right in front of me. A heavy silence descends.

Does she expect me to offer praise as well?

I love to praise, but only when women are on their knees, submission in their eyes.

"You're in my way," she finally says, and a part of me wants to react, but I control myself.

I give her a curt nod, my jaw set tight, and she quickly glances at a tattoo on my neck before brushing past me. Lexy follows closely behind, and I fall in after them.

Colin and Dean, the security personnel I'd outmaneuvered on my first day, join me in the staff green room as we await Victoria's arrival. Their eyes widen, taking in the spread of food laid out before them.

"You're not eating?" Colin inquires, noticing only a cup of coffee in front of me.

"No."

"A man of few words?" Dean questions, piling his plate with carbs and other food that, in my professional opinion, might hinder his reaction time in an emergency situation.

"You could say that," I respond, finishing off the last of my espresso.

"Listen, it was nothing personal yesterday. I just had to prove to her the holes in her security detail," I explain, wanting to make my motives clear.

"I see," Dean replies, a trace of disdain in his voice. His expression changes, though, as curiosity takes over. "We looked you up, you know. Your background. It's pretty impressive, to say the least. Medals, commendations... but what happened with your team? They say everyone died but you."

I stiffen at the question, memories I've long tried to suppress threatening to surface. I didn't expect my past to be a topic of conversation, and I certainly don't want to dwell on it now.

"That's behind me," I say curtly, not wishing to elaborate.

"But surely you can tell us a bit more," Colin chimes in, clearly in awe of my credentials. "I mean, you were a hero. Your medals prove that. Why leave it all behind?"

I look at the two of them, seeing the genuine interest in their eyes but also recognizing that some stories are better left untold, buried in the past.

"I did what I had to do. Now I'm here, doing this job," I respond, my voice firm.

Thankfully, they seem to take the hint, falling into a respectful silence.

My past is something I've moved on from, but their questions have a way of bringing it all back. The medals mean nothing when weighed against the loss and the choices I had to make. Now, my focus is on the job at hand, protecting Victoria and ensuring her safety.

But the memories linger, a reminder of where I've been and what I have left behind.

4
VICTORIA

Hair and makeup have morphed me into a megastar that I barely recognize.

My hair is set in Hollywood curls, and I'm adorned in a red satin dress that perfectly accentuates my natural curves. With my chalk-white skin and red lips, I bear a striking resemblance to Jessica Rabbit. I like this version of me. This brand, this persona that has been crafted for me, is something I've grown to embrace. My record label and an exceptional team of stylists have sculpted me into a jazzy, soulful artist who embodies the essence of a sexy siren.

Everyone has left my room, and I have just about two minutes before I need to go on stage. I take some calming breaths to settle my normal jitters before performing in front of thousands. I've been here before and learned to use my nerves to my advantage, but lately, it hasn't been working all too well, and they have been getting the best of me.

Closing my eyes, I revel in the fantasy. I imagine myself singing in front of tens of thousands of fans, feeling the rush of excitement and contentment as if it's what I was born to do. The screaming fans are all there for me, chanting my name. But then, something in the fantasy shifts. The screaming morphs into my own cries, and I see a different image entirely. It's me, but in the reflection of my own eyes after being abducted and rescued. My face is streaked with blood, my wrists red and raw from their restraints.

"No!" I yell out, my eyes snapping open, blazing with fear while I try to push the terrible memory away.

Immediately, the door to my dressing room swings open, and there stands Kingsley, concern etched across his face.

"Is everything all right, Miss Slater?" Kingsley asks, his eyes quickly scanning the room, assessing for any possible threats.

I feel a blush of embarrassment coloring my cheeks. "Yes... yes... I'm fine," I stammer, trying to regain my composure.

His eyes linger on me for a moment longer, seeming to see right through my flimsy excuse. But then he nods, accepting my explanation. "I'll be right outside," he assures me, starting to turn away.

"Wait," I call after him, a sudden impulse taking over me. "Aren't you going to wish me good luck?"

He pauses, his eyes returning to mine, a hint of amusement in his gaze. "Luck is for the ill-prepared, and you are *very* prepared," he says, his eyes roaming over my body in a way that sends a thrill of anticipation through me.

I don't know why, but something propels me to approach him. Maybe because I need to forget about the image that plagues me. Nevertheless, I find myself strutting toward him, my hips swinging flirtatiously.

A part of me wants to provoke him, to misbehave right in front of him. I want to challenge him, to see how far I can push this dominating side of him. Not many people dare to speak to me that way, and it's different. I find myself drawn to it, ready to engage with this new dynamic.

I stop just a breath away from him, our eyes locking, the air between us charged with tension. Dark brown eyes stare down at me, and it's a daring game, a battle of wills, and neither of us is backing down.

"I hope you're ready for tonight's performance," I say, my voice dripping with feigned innocence, my eyes never leaving his.

"Miss Slater, I am ready for any and all eventualities." His response is a slow, knowing smile, and I realize that the game is on.

He's up to the challenge, and so am I.

Let the show begin.

Tonight, I'm on an Australian television show before we jet off.

I'm still dancing on a cloud from my performance in front of a sold-out arena of fifty-thousand people, riding on a wave of adrenaline from one interview to the next. Only four hours of sleep, but it doesn't bother me. I will sleep on the plane tonight on my way to a two-day vacation in Italy. My team is flying back to LAX while I continue on to Sardinia for my brother Vincent's engagement party. Unfortunately, Kingsley will be with me.

I'm mid-text to my soon-to-be sister-in-law, Rosie, when Lexy walks in holding a piece of paper. "Here's the list of questions the panel of journalists will ask," she informs me, her tone insistent while my hairdresser, Toni, puts the final touches on my hair.

"I don't want to know, Lexy. You know that," I reply, shooing the paper away.

"It's live TV, Viki. You should be prepared," she counters, her voice tinged with worry.

"I'm not worried," I say, dismissing her concern. "You've briefed them on what they can't ask, so why worry? I let out a deep exhale, tiredness creeping in. " I have enough to worry about."

I look up and catch Kingsley's reflection in the mirror of my dressing room, stationed like the bodyguard he is. Our eyes meet, and something in his gaze holds my attention. *Why do I find myself wanting him to look at me with the same dominant intensity he had in my dressing room before the show?*

"What do you know about Kingsley?" I ask Lexy, keeping my voice low, curiosity getting the better of me.

"Apart from the fact that he's drop-dead gorgeous but could also strangle me with one hand?" Lexy teases, her eyes twinkling.

"Jesus, Lexy," I admonish, trying to keep a straight face.

"I wouldn't mind if he strangled me," Toni adds and nods with a moan that makes us all laugh out loud.

I continue to study Kingsley's reflection as Lexy answers, drawing me back to the conversation. "Well, I only know what Vincent has told us," she says, her voice serious now. "He's one of the best in the business, a real professional. Ex-Special Forces, I think. He's got a reputation for being tight-lipped and stern, but he's the best at what he does."

I turn my attention back to Lexy, considering her words. "That's it?" I ask, feeling a twinge of disappointment. "Nothing more personal? No family, friends, background?"

Lexy shakes her head, her expression apologetic. "I'm afraid not. He's a private person from what I've gathered. Keeps his personal life separate from his professional life."

I chew on my lip, feeling both frustrated and intrigued. The lack of information only adds to the mystery surrounding Kingsley, fueling my curiosity. "So he's good at his job," I say slowly, my mind working. "But what about the way he treats people? The fans, the staff? He seems... intense."

Lexy's eyes flicker to Kingsley's reflection, and she hesitates for a moment before answering. "Yes, he's intense, but that's part of what makes him good at what he does. In the few days he's been here, he's not afraid to make tough decisions if it means keeping you safe. But it's you who needs to trust him, Viki. Without that, you won't have a professional relationship at all."

Her words resonate with me, echoing my own thoughts. I feel a strange connection to Kingsley, a desire to uncover the man behind the façade. But I also know he's here to do a job, and I need to respect his boundaries.

I nod at Lexy, signaling the end of our conversation, and turn my attention back to my incoming text. But while the minutes tick by, and the time for my live interview draws near, I can't help but steal glances at Kingsley, wondering what secrets he's hiding and whether I'll ever get the chance to discover them.

The live studio audience's laughter fills the room, and their excitement is palpable. I revel in the energy, holding them captivated as the interview nears the end. My mind, however, drifts to the upcoming vacation, complete with relaxing lavender eye masks, prosecco, and Italian food. After a grueling few months on tour, the thought of rest is intoxicating.

"And we are back in five... four... three..." the studio hand counts us in from the ad break, the teleprompter rolling smoothly.

"And we're back with singing sensation, Viki Slate, who has taken the world by storm! She's just been on tour, and everyone is dying to know when we can expect her next album to drop. The anticipation is crazy," the host, Martin, exclaims.

The audience's shrieks fill the studio.

"Well, I'll be back in LA after this, and we'll start laying down the second half of the album then. I'd have to get back to you on a date, but I can assure you it's worth the hype," I reply, feeling the audience's enthusiasm.

"Oh, we can't wait, can we?" a female journalist chimes in, captivating the audience once again, drawing applause.

"Now, I know you have to jet off, but can we try something new with you?" Martin asks, his eyes twinkling with curiosity.

I swallow roughly but answer confidently, "Sure."

"Because we have such a fan-frenzied audience, I'd like to throw the mic for a question. Would you be willing to take a question from your fans?" he asks, his gaze fixed on me.

"Of course. I wouldn't be here without my fans," I respond, sincerity lacing my voice.

"Excellent... who do we have?" Martin inquires, and all eyes cast to the dark audience.

A stagehand brings a microphone to a man in the back row. It's dim, and I can barely make him out.

"Yes, sir. What would you like to ask Viki Slate?" Martin asks.

Silence. "Does your abduction stay with you? Haunt you

in the quiet nights?" The question comes unexpectedly and chilling.

My breath catches in my throat, fear trailing down my spine. My eyes dart to the side of the stage, where Lexy stares back at me, shocked. Kingsley, eyes narrow, whispers something into his radio.

"You don't have to answer that," the journalist says, a touch of concern in his voice.

I clear my throat, regaining my composure. "What happened to me... I don't wish upon anyone, but it's only made me stronger," I say, voice steady, but inside, my emotions are near breaking.

My chest constricts, my breathing hitches, the shadows of the past threatening to break through.

And with that, the interview comes to a close. I'm smiling, but I feel like I'm outside my body— a spectator in the room. I am not listening, but a static of voices surround me, and the producer counts down until the credits roll.

"I'm sorry, Viki, we didn't realize..." Martin's voice trails off, but I don't hear the rest of his apology. I stand abruptly, fear and anxiety clawing at me, making me feel lightheaded as I practically run out of the studio.

I make it to the green room and shut the door, leaving Lexy and Kingsley on the other side.

A loud knock pulls me from the depths of my mind.

"I just need a minute," I yell back at them, lying on the sofa, trying to regulate my breathing.

The question about my abduction caught me entirely off guard. After the first time I was asked about it in an interview, I'd put a stop to any more personal questions. Lexy always briefs interviewers on topics that are off-limits, and this one is strictly off-limits. But an audience member asking? That was completely unexpected.

The question has triggered a wave of anxiety I can't seem to control. My heart pounds in my chest, and my mind races, replaying the memories I've tried to put behind me.

I hear a firm knock at the door. "Miss Slater? May I come in?" Kingsley's voice is loud and authoritative. Weirdly, it brings me comfort.

I hesitate for a moment, then call out, "Yes."

The door opens, and Kingsley steps inside, his eyes searching my face.

5

KINGSLEY

My eyes lock with hers, and I see vulnerability shimmering there. Miss Slater rises from her seat, leaning against her dresser for support.

This would be the moment to ask if she's all right after that distressing question that she so blatantly struggled to answer. It's a fear I've witnessed in men on the verge of death or soldiers traumatized from the horrors of battle. Instead, I take a moment to look at those striking blue eyes and auburn hair cascading in curls down her back. Her petite frame might deceive some, but not me.

"What is it?" she asks, attempting to regain her posture, but I've learned not to be fooled by her size. She's brimming with sass and confidence, and she's headstrong. Most celebrities are, or so I've been told by my employer, who handles security for many A-listers.

"I've got Dean and Colin looking for the audience member, but he left when the show ended."

"He was just a fan, curious, that's all," she replies, dismissing me.

"However, as far as I'm aware, your abductors remain at large."

She shudders, then tries to mask it with a forced gesture, but I catch it. Reading body language is second nature to me.

"That was in Tokyo. We're in Australia now," she snaps back, her tone dripping with defiance.

Has she not heard of worldwide organized crime syndicates?

Suppressing my frustration, I step closer. Our proximity is such that she has to tilt her head to meet my gaze. "I notice everything, Miss Slater. Every single detail. We need to remain vigilant."

Her breathing becomes slightly uneven while I'm enveloped by her scent—a mix of woody cinnamon and floral notes. Were she not so defiant, her beauty would be truly breathtaking.

She steps closer, the satin of her dress brushing against me. The outline of her figure makes me tense up. "So do I, Kingsley," she murmurs, and the way my name rolls off her tongue sends my imagination down a dark path.

"We have a plane to catch," I manage to say, keeping my voice steady.

A hint of a smile tugs at her lips as if she's conquered a challenge. There's a fire in her ocean eyes, a spark of defiance. She may have won this round, but it's far from over.

Lexy's entrance breaks the mounting tension between us. "I'm so sorry, Viki," she says, and I instinctively distance myself from her, walking just outside the room but still in earshot.

"Are you okay?" Lexy inquires. Miss Slater's attention is now solely on Lexy, the earlier tension momentarily forgotten. "I don't know why they allowed an audience question.

They shouldn't have. We won't be returning here. They're blacklisted, I just told the producer."

Miss Slater's retort is sharp. "I'm not exactly thrilled!"

I'm curious about her abduction. While I've read the police report and even received a summary from her brother, Vincent, hearing it directly from her would provide a different perspective. But, I wasn't employed to solve a crime.

I am her bodyguard, assigned to protect her for the next six months.

My mind drifts to my past, recalling the unfortunate mission where I was the sole survivor. Trying to shake off those thoughts, I reenter the room. "We need to leave," I announce more sharply than I had intended.

Lexy shoots me a glare. "Could you try having a bit of compassion?"

"I have a feeling Kingsley's heart might just be a bit cold," Miss Slater interjects, her gaze piercing.

Enraged, I can barely contain my emotions, but my training kicks in, and I manage a tight-lipped smile. "Are you ready to depart?"

Her stare is challenging, and Lexy sighs in exasperation.

"Your luggage is on the plane. Enjoy Italy, and I'll see you back in LA," Lexy says and hugs her boss.

"Thanks, Lexy," she replies.

"And, Viki, try to relax," Lexy adds with a hint of mischief. "Who knows, you might find an enchanting Italian man."

Viki giggles, then fixes her eyes on me. "Perhaps someone with a touch of warmth in his soul."

The jet's interior is adorned with rich wood, mahogany panels, spacious leather seats, and tables. Taking in the opulent surroundings, I flashback to the terrain of the Somalian hills, where my only luxuries were my medical kit, gun, and rucksack. Despite the luxury, I can't ignore the fact that it's just the two of us on this twenty-two-hour flight to Sardinia.

The flight attendant greets us cordially, and the pilot initiates takeoff, but they both retreat to their quarters for rest. This leaves me ample time to go over the security measures in Sardinia, scrutinize the villa's layout, and familiarize myself with the schematics of the restaurant where Victoria's brother and Rosie plan to celebrate their engagement.

I've liaised with the local security, alerting them of Victoria's arrival, and received a rudimentary schedule from her brother and Rosie, which is useful. The main hitch I've encountered is the accommodation arrangement.

Victoria's villa is farther from mine than I would have preferred. My request for a neighboring bungalow was denied since other VIPs have already claimed them. Though I'm only three bungalows away, it's an oversight I hadn't anticipated, and it unsettles me. I remind myself, however, that the details of her visit to Italy are confidential, known only to her team and family. Consequently, the odds of a security breach are relatively low. Still, I can't completely shake off the lingering concern.

The flight attendant approaches me. "Mr. Kingsley, we will be refueling shortly in Singapore. Can I offer you a beverage?"

"No, thank you," I reply.

The bedroom door opens behind me, but I don't need to turn around to know it's Miss Slater.

"Are you sure I can't tempt you?" the flight attendant flirts. She's attractive with her tall, curvaceous figure. Her eyes wander toward my V-neck shirt, revealing my tattoos.

"I'm sure," I confirm, giving her a courteous smile, and her gaze then shifts to Miss Slater.

"Miss Slate, can I offer you a beverage before we start our descent into Singapore?" Her tone is noticeably more respectful and less flirty than before.

"A green tea, please," Miss Slater responds, taking a seat across from me.

"Of course," the attendant replies, retreating to prepare the drink.

Miss Slater's gaze immediately lands on my shoulder and neck. Seeing me in a T-shirt is a novelty for her since I've mostly worn my uniform of pants and a dress shirt. She tilts her head, studying the ink. "What are they of?" she inquires.

I catch a glimpse of her, clad in a skirt and a crop top. Her midriff, a tantalizing display of creamy skin, is exposed. But I ensure that my gaze stays locked with hers. Her makeup has been wiped clean, and her tousled hair suggests she's taken a nap.

"It's a desert," I respond, keeping the explanation brief, not keen to delve into the details.

"A desert?" she echoes just as the attendant sets her drink in front of her.

"Thank you," I address the attendant, who responds with a flirtatious smile. I think Miss Slater notices, but she remains silent.

"And what else?" Miss Slater questions, sipping her drink through the straw, her eyes fixed on me.

"It's the terrain of Somalia."

"Is that where you earned your medals?" she asks, and

I'm surprised she's dug into my background. "I like to know who's working so closely with me, Kingsley."

"I see."

"Although all I know is that you earned three medals for... a quick Google search of 'Kingsley Williams' says that you were the sole survivor of your team. So what's the story there?"

My lips press into a thin line. *Is there no escape from my past?*

"I don't want to talk about it," I say, attempting to maintain a professional distance.

"We may as well get to know each other. We have another thirteen hours on this plane stuck together."

She has a point. Still, I don't like it. I don't like sharing. I don't like experiencing these emotions.

"Two years ago, I led a team of four Special Forces men. We were on a mission to rescue an invaded village from militia when it all went wrong."

She leans back in her chair, a genuine interest lighting her features. "I'm sorry," she offers, and her sincerity catches me off guard. "What happened?"

"It doesn't matter. My team was killed, and I was the only survivor. Apparently, that deserves a medal," I say, staring out the window in disbelief. "Fucking ridiculous," I mutter under my breath.

The attendant reappears, breaking the raw moment of genuine conversation between us. "We are starting our descent into Changi. Can you please fasten your seat belts?"

I nod at her and return my gaze to Miss Slater, who is looking at me pensively. For once, I can't decipher her body language.

"You've caught someone's eye," she states, breaking the silence with a sly smile, clearly indicating the attendant.

As the plane begins its descent, I cock an inquisitive eyebrow. "Not a concern," I respond, nonchalantly brushing off her remark. "We'll remain on board while they refuel, then we're airborne again at one p.m."

"All right," she replies, her thoughtful gaze shifting to the window.

I've reviewed security at the hotel while she's been glued to her laptop, and an hour later, we're back in the sky. Victoria is preoccupied with her computer, and only when we're soaring above the clouds again does she start to huff and puff in frustration.

"Clearly, something is bothering you, Miss Slater. What's the issue?" I ask, her restlessness preventing my attempt at a nap.

"Seriously? What the hell?" she shouts. My eyes snap open. Sleep now a lost cause.

"What's the matter?" I probe, sitting upright.

"Those idiots," she seethes, completely ignoring me.

"For goodness sake, are you going to share?" I ask impatiently.

She glares up from her screen, her eyes ablaze. "Don't you dare start," she warns, then thrusts her laptop in my direction.

The headline blinds me. "*Viki Slate Like a Deer in Headlights.*" I swiftly skim the article, which portrays her as an unsuspecting trauma victim. From the question the man in the audience asked, I can see why she's irritated, but it could have been worse.

She crosses her arms defensively. "Mariel," she summons the flight attendant. "I'll have a double scotch," she orders, her hand trembling slightly, pushing it into her arm, trying to conceal it.

"Do you genuinely believe that alcohol is the solution?"

I question. Even though it's like the pot calling the kettle black, I'm more concerned about her well-being than my own.

"Save me the speech, Kingsley. How would you like this splashed about the news, huh? You have no idea what I have to put up with from the media. One minute, they're romantically linking me with a singer I've met once, or they're hating on a dress I wore to the Grammys. Now this? This article portrays me like I am weak and fragile from my kidnapping."

Mariel puts a full tumbler of amber liquid in front of her.

"I'm not drinking alone. Get him a glass too," she orders before I can even object.

She glances in my direction, then quickly moves to fulfill her request.

"You're off duty now," she declares with a tight sigh. I watch, both impressed and taken aback while she downs the entire glass in one gulp. "I mean, do they think the readers would be more interested in my album hitting number one in five countries? No, that doesn't make headlines."

She slams down the empty glass.

"Here you go, sir." Mariel hands me my drink and wisely chooses that moment to leave.

"Just ignore it," I suggest, attempting to quell her fiery disposition.

She puffs out her cheeks, then looks over her shoulder. "Mariel, keep them coming," she demands.

She turns to find me shaking my head. "We have plenty of time to sober up on this long-haul flight. Or are you scared of something?" she presses, a challenging glint in her eyes that makes my skin crawl with heat.

"I fear nothing," I reply, downing the drink in a single gulp.

Her blue eyes lower to my Adam's apple, and as I swallow, I silently acknowledge my acceptance of her challenge. I know I shouldn't, but I also know my limits. My years of training won't deter me from a little challenge.

"You shouldn't read that stuff about you," I say. "Especially if it's click-bait rubbish anyway."

"But it's like telling a child Santa's real and leaving it at that. The kid always wants to know more, the what, how, why... that's how I am. When something's written about me, I need to know."

"Why?" I ask, genuinely curious. "Why does it matter?"

"Don't you care about what people think of you?" she counters.

"No," I reply bluntly. "Couldn't give a fuck, Miss Slater."

She shakes her head, "Public opinion can make or break a career," she reasons, snatching another glass of scotch from Mariel's tray and knocking it back.

"Slow down, Miss Slater," I caution her, observing this petite woman consuming more alcohol than her frame can likely handle.

"Everyone usually calls me Viki or Miss Slate," she declares, finishing off her drink.

"Well, I'm not everyone. I prefer to call you by your legal name." I'm quick with my reply when another glass of scotch is placed in front of me.

As she licks the last bit of scotch off her lip, I find myself momentarily distracted by the action.

"Are you married, Kingsley?" she questions further, her curiosity evident.

I shake my head.

"Gay?"

I nearly choke on my scotch. This woman certainly has balls. "Excuse me?" I question in case I heard her incorrectly.

"Are you gay or something?" she prods, a teasing smile playing on her lips.

"No, Miss Slater, I'm not gay," I respond, my fingers curling tightly around my tumbler.

She shrugs her shoulder, "You're old enough to be married or with a partner..."

"I'm thirty-four and certainly not old. I like being single, being alone." I level her with a pointed stare, hoping she stops the personal inquisition. Then I lift the glass of scotch and drain it, savoring the fiery trail it leaves down my throat.

"No attachments. How very Special Forces of you," she teases.

"Exactly," I respond, keeping my voice steady. "Attachments can be lethal in the field."

"But we're not in the field, Kingsley," she so clearly points out.

Is she flirting with me?

God, if she weren't my boss, I punish her with my itchy palm.

"I maintain a strict boundary between my personal and professional life, Miss Slater."

"Well, if you want to continue working for me, you'll have to bend that rule," she says, popping an olive into her mouth with seductive ease.

"Pardon?" I manage to stutter out.

"Oh, not like that," she clarifies with a dismissive wave of her hand. "I can't handle having a robot around me, Kingsley. You're here because you're obviously the best. Just loosen up a bit, will you?"

My immediate relief is met with curiosity as to why she immediately dismissed me. "I'll try, *Miss Slater*."

"Viki," she corrects.

"That's not going to happen, Miss Slater."

"Fine. How are you with poker?" she asks, producing a deck of cards from her handbag.

"Do you always keep a deck in there?" I ask, a hint of amusement creeping into my voice.

Her smile broadens. "Is that a smile, Kingsley?" she teases, clearly pleased with herself.

"No."

She narrows her eyes and smirks, "You didn't answer my question."

"I'm a master," I say confidently. "Now deal."

6

VICTORIA

Kingsley seems to have loosened up, his controlling demeanor softening. A part of me is strangely drawn to this aspect of him. Feeling surprisingly at ease, I can't help but admit I'm having fun.

"Two pairs," he announces, grinning slyly. "Beat that, Miss Slater."

I chuckle, knowing what hand I'm holding, and he's completely oblivious to his impending loss.

He quirks an eyebrow at me, his impatience bubbling to the surface. I lick my bottom lip, suppressing a satisfied giggle. "Well, Kingsley, seems like you've been outplayed again." I place my winning hand on the table.

"Jesus Christ." He exhales. "A royal flush," he mutters, disbelieving. "Are you sure you're not hiding an ace anywhere?" he teases, his gaze lowering to my T-shirt.

"I assure you I'm not," I reply. "But feel free to frisk me," I add cheekily.

His eyes darken, and I'm drawn to them. I've been so forward around him, so flirty—an unexpected side of me that's beginning to surface. I haven't felt this animated around a man since the assault a few months ago. "Cat got your tongue?" I continue to prod him because, well, why not? I've lost count of how many scotches I have had, and this seems way more fun.

"Of course not," he responds. "I'm just curious... how much do you enjoy being a brat?"

"Whoa!" I reply, reaching for my drink. "Finally, he says what's on his mind."

When did I change to champagne?

Before I can lift it, his hand is on my wrist, closing around it. "I think you've had enough to drink," he cautions.

But I slip out of his grasp, trailing my hand up his arm, tracing the sinewy veins and the intricate tattoos covering his muscular forearm. I hear his sharp intake of breath when I let my fingers wander further up to his biceps. Leaning closer, I continue my exploration, surprised he hasn't stopped me yet. I continue tracing a path up his arm until I reach the edge of his shirt sleeve. There's a boldness in me that I haven't felt in a long while, and I want to keep exploring. With an impish grin, I decide to be a bit more daring.

Without breaking eye contact, I hoist myself up from my seat, delicately climbing onto the table separating us. The look of surprise in Kingsley's eyes is priceless, but he doesn't make a move to stop me. Instead, his gaze follows me, a peculiar blend of curiosity and alarm in his eyes. It's clear that he didn't expect this, but then again, neither did I.

Once comfortably situated on the table, I continue my earlier expedition. My fingers glide across the broad expanse of his shoulders, my movements unhurried. With each passing second, the tension in the air between us thickens. I feel fearless and in control for the first time in a long while. And I can tell by the way Kingsley watches me he isn't quite sure what to make of this bold, daring side of me. But for now, that doesn't matter. Right now, at this moment, I am thoroughly enjoying this exhilarating game of poker.

It's too late to change what happens next. I widen my legs, my skirt raises high on my thighs, and I lower myself onto him. He quickly sets his hands roughly on my hips in the exposed part, and I shiver at the connection.

He grabs me and pulls me close so our lips are almost touching, then lets out a low growl that hits me somewhere low. "Stop," he says.

"Or what?" I challenge, tipsy, thinking riding this body-guard will be the perfect distraction I need right now. I feel him swell underneath me. Holy fuck, he's *big*.

As I reach to caress his face, a fleeting desire of vulnera-bility sweeping over me, he's swift to intercept. My fingers are halted, mere millimeters from the well-defined curve of his lips and the strong line of his jaw. That jaw clenches as he holds my hand firmly. "You're drunk. You don't want this," he declares, the hint of a warning in his voice.

"How would you know what I want?" I snap back. The sharpness in my voice, a result of the sting of his rejection, surprises even me.

In a display of his sheer strength, he scoops me up effortlessly, my feet dangling off the floor. The closeness provides a clearer view of his rugged features. God, he's even more stunning up close.

"I know what I want," he counters, setting me down

gently yet with finality. There's a gravity to his words, a deeper meaning I can't quite decipher. "And it's not my boss."

Ouch.

He turns around and strides to a seat far from me. My ego, volatile and brimming, refuses to let him off that easy. I'm well aware that the fiery, defiant side he's witnessing isn't my usual demeanor. But how dare he? He's evoked something raw in me, a side I wasn't even aware existed.

I follow him, intent on continuing our charged exchange, but he whirls around, cornering me against the cabin's wall. My heart hammers in my chest, the world spinning momentarily from the abruptness of the move.

"Sleep it off, Miss Slater." His tone is gruff, yet I detect a hint of concern.

His eyes, intense, burn into mine. I hold his gaze then as it flits down to my lips, my breath catches, the air between us thick with tension. Overwhelmed, I close the distance, my lips brushing against his cold ones, just a ghost of a touch. But it's enough. The world starts to blur at the edges.

I can hear him call out, but his voice sounds distant like he's miles away. Slowly, my legs give way, and the last thing I remember is the feel of strong arms catching me before everything fades away.

The deep, commanding voice calls out my name, the same voice I recall from my dream. While I struggle to hold on to the remnants of that dream, the voice becomes more insistent, and the sensation of a warm hand grasping mine pulls me further to consciousness.

"Miss Slater."

My eyes flutter open and slam into Kingsley's concerned gaze. The harsh cabin light assaults my senses, and a throbbing headache ensues. "Oh God," I groan out, pressing a hand to my temple.

He stands upright, looking refreshingly unaffected by the previous nine hours. The memories of our poker game, me on the table, lowering myself on his lap... oh fuck.

Before I can dwell on it, his stance draws my attention. Arms crossed, muscles evident beneath his fitted black T-shirt, he exudes an air of amused superiority.

Wincing, I snap, "Wipe that smug look off your face and get me some Advil. It's in the side pocket of my bag."

He quirks a thick eyebrow, then rummages through my bag, and when he resurfaces, he's holding two familiar bottles. My eyes widen in realization. *Shit.*

"This explains a lot," he says, ignoring the aspirin and eyeing the bottle of Valium. "You're petite, but even then, it must've taken more than alcohol to knock you out cold for the remainder of the flight."

"Thank you, Dr. Kingsley. I'd like my Advil now," I reply, my tone dripping with sarcasm.

Not registering that, he continues, "How many did you take?" He grips the Valium bottle a bit tighter, clearly intent on getting an answer.

I sigh exasperatedly. "Two, okay? I hate flying. Can you please hand over the bottle now before I keel over?"

He offers me the Advil with a tight expression and a glass of water, which I gratefully accept. When I down the pills, I recall my little lie. Ever since my traumatic abduction, Valium has been a crutch for my rampant anxiety. It's not just about flying. It's about existing without panic. Without the little helpers, I feel I can't get through the day sometimes. But Kingsley doesn't need to know any of this. Why would he?

"The car's waiting for us," Kingsley says curtly, already making his way down the plane's staircase.

A pang of guilt gnaws at me, watching him retreat. What on earth did I do to upset him this much? Determined to amend things, I follow him down. This trip is my escape, a much-needed break, and I don't want any lingering tension with Kingsley, especially since we got off to a rocky start.

Emerging from the plane, the afternoon sun graces my face. The warmth is a sharp contrast to the icy atmosphere between Kingsley and me. After the pilot bids me a good journey, I spot a sleek car waiting on the tarmac.

Despite his mood, Kingsley stands at the door and waits for me to settle into the back seat before firmly shutting the door. I'm slightly disappointed when he doesn't join me and sits up front next to the driver. I really must have pissed him off.

The driver tips his hat in my direction and offers a warm greeting, "*Buona sera, Signorina Slater.*"

I muster a smile, attempting not to let my concern about Kingsley's demeanor show. However, any hope of clearing the air diminishes when Kingsley glances at me briefly in the rear vision mirror, then flicks his attention forward.

"Let's go," he says tersely, and the car starts to move.

Amidst a stifling silence from Kingsley and an impromptu history lesson about Sardinia from Giancarlo, our talkative driver, we reach a slice of paradise in less than an hour. Kingsley takes care of the check-in, and we're promptly whisked away to my bungalow in a slick motorized buggy.

The setting sun splashes the sky with purple and soft pink hues while the villas are covered in cascades of vibrant bougainvilleas. Each villa boasts a plunge pool that leads to a private beach with the bluest water I've ever seen.

This place is exactly what I need.

Ever the security expert, Kingsley sweeps the bungalow before I can enter. His diligence might seem excessive, given our low profile, but maybe my previous guards had been too relaxed. The mere thought tugs at my heartstrings, igniting a surge of emotion. I can't help but question if my entire ordeal might have taken a more hopeful turn had Kingsley been by my side from the very beginning.

"All clear," he confirms, stepping aside to let me pass.

The bungalow's interior takes my breath away. Rich green plants brighten the corners while the wooden parquet flooring and plush linen furniture create an air of luxury. A grand four-poster bed draped in pristine white linens tempts me from the master suite. Succumbing to its allure, I sink into the bed as a delicate rose fragrance envelops me.

Kingsley's throat-clearing from the doorway draws my attention. "My villa is three doors down to the south. I'll be back in an hour," he announces.

Feeling a pang of guilt, I sit up. "Sorry if I made you uncomfortable."

His expression softens. "Let's just forget about it," he replies, the corners of his mouth pulling into a slight smile.

I'm so relieved he's handling this professionally and with more maturity than me.

"Deal. See you in an hour then. We'll find my family."

He gives a curt nod, adding, "You have my number if you need anything."

With that, he steps out, leaving me in solitude. I push away the fear that begins to gnaw at me when I'm alone, threatening to take over my relaxation. When the Advil starts to kick in, I grab my phone and dial Julius' number.

While Vincent is likely caught up in engagement party preparations with Rosie, Julius has always been my go-to due in part to our closeness in age. At least by calling someone, I won't feel alone and be left with my thoughts.

I'm just about to hang up when he answers the call. "Victoria!"

"Julius. Where is everyone?" I ask.

"We're here in our suite. Are you here?"

"Yes, I'm here! I'm waiting at the restaurant! Get your asses down here." Okay, that was a slight lie, but I know my brother, and he takes forever.

Julius chuckles. "All right, we'll see you shortly."

After a hot, invigorating shower and a refreshing liter of water, I'm buzzing with anticipation to reunite with my family and meet Julius' new wife, Isabella. I opt for a breezy halter-neck sundress and pair it with wedge heels. As I apply a touch of lip gloss, a knock at the door punctuates the air. Considering it's exactly seven p.m., there's no guessing who's on the other side.

Kingsley's gaze travels over me when I open the door, taking in every detail. The journey of his eyes is deliberate, and by the time they meet mine, I sense a hint of appreciation. Yet, his staunch posture gives nothing away.

While part of me is tempted to probe for a compliment, I refrain. One bout of embarrassment around him today is more than enough.

"Nice dress, Miss Slater," he comments, and I'm nearly bowled over.

"Thank you, Kingsley." I smile and suppress my instinct to reply cheekily.

We exit the bungalow, he secures the door behind us, and I catch a deep intake of breath from him.

"That might be the nicest thing you've said to me since we began working together," I remark, unable to keep my playful side at bay entirely.

He lets out a soft chuckle, shaking his head slightly. "It's a surprise to me too." There's no real edge to his voice, just a hint of amusement

7

KINGSLEY

As the day dawns, the raw beauty of this place is everywhere I turn. The golden sunlight dances on the lush greenery, casting enchanting shadows. But beneath that calm, an old soldier's instincts stir.

Running ten miles every morning keeps me sharp, alert, and more importantly, sane. I decide to cool down with a walk, patrolling her villa. The undisturbed shutters hang low, and she's probably deep in sleep. The tranquility of the scene contrasts with the faint unease that gnaws at me, reminding me of the ever-present need to stay vigilant.

After a brisk shower, I step into my usual attire of black fitted cargo pants and a matching polo. I tuck my gun at the back of my pants and pull my shirt over it to conceal it.

Outside her room, anticipation mixes with duty. I knock loudly on her wooden door, the pungent bougainvillea flowers filling the air.

She opens the door with a whoosh, her auburn hair flying back like she's in a hair care commercial. "Good morning, Kingsley."

A smile beams across her pretty face, and her fleeting

gaze lowers to my neck tattoos. I like the way she looks at them like she *really* looks at them.

"Good morning, Miss Slater."

The silence that follows is charged. She holds the door open in a red strappy dress, cleavage out and creamy thighs. She breaks the tension, clearing her throat, ensuring my focus remains where it should.

Goddamn, Williams, get your shit together.

"Will you take me now?" she teasingly asks. *What?* Before my mind races down a dangerous path, she clarifies, "Into town, Kingsley."

Holding back my thoughts, I manage to say, "Yes, of course. Let's go." My voice comes out gravelly, lower than I intended.

Their shopping? Jesus, fuck. It's almost as intense as some operations I've been on.

In the heart of Sardinia's shopping district, boutiques line the streets with displays of the season's finest. The women—Rosie, Isabella, Victoria, and her mother, Tatianna—shuffle between stores, their laughter and enthusiasm painful.

Now, I'm standing in the corner at a high-end dress shop, holding the wall up like I have in all nine stores before this one. The interior of the store is awash with soft lighting, illuminating racks adorned with a myriad of colors, designs, and fabrics.

The women seem to really like this store, especially as their voices have shrieked an octave higher each time they pick up a new garment off the rack. Tatianna, however, appears thoughtful, her fingers delicately trailing over the silken fabrics, like she's present but not really. I wonder if it has anything to do with last night's dinner and the obvious strain between her and her husband and her husband and three children—Vincent, Julius, and Victoria.

After a short while, the curtain of a changing room whisks open, revealing Rosie in a scarlet evening number. She walks across the store to where Isabella emerges from the other changing room in a flowing azure gown.

"Oh my gosh, aren't you both stunning!" Tatianna gushes when she motions for them to spin around.

"Kingsley?" I hear Miss Slater call from the changing room nearest to me. Her voice is muffled slightly by the curtain of her changing stall, so I peel my head around just enough so I'm not intruding. "Could you..." she hesitates for a fraction of a second, her eyes avoiding mine, "... help with the zipper?"

I can only see the top of her head and bare shoulders when I peer inside. The dress she is trying on hangs loosely, its zipper undone.

Goddamn, is there not anyone else who can do this? I exhale, then quickly walk inside the stall, reminding myself of the boundaries as I step inside. The cubicle is small, her scent everywhere, a mix of floral notes and something uniquely hers filling the small space.

My jaw ticks when her black lace bra that is hanging up comes into view. The delicate skin of her back is warm under my fingers, and for a brief moment, the world outside ceases to exist. Carefully grasping the zipper, the room becomes static with tension. The zipper slides up smoothly, sealing the dress against her form.

"Thank you," she whispers, her voice soft and vulnerable. I can only nod, my throat suddenly dry. She turns and looks up at me. "What were you and Vincent talking about last night before dinner?"

I try not to look down at the curves of her breasts in my line of sight and focus on the question.

"He was asking about security at your house and the protocols I've established since starting."

Hmm."

"Hmm?" I echo, feeling so close to her in the changing room but unable to move.

"My brother can be very overprotective."

"Because he loves you."

"I guess so."

A charged pause swirls between us, and I see her neck suck in a deep breath.

"I should go," I say, breaking whatever the hell that was.

"Before you do... tell me," she says, stepping back slightly. "What do you think?" she asks, standing in front of me, wearing a stunning blue dress that curves her in all the right places.

"It's nice," I manage to say, and she turns toward me, her eyes wide. "Oh? I love it." She frowns, clearly disheartened. "Maybe it doesn't look as good as I think it does." She spins around, and I can't help but notice how the dress hugs the curves of her backside.

Kingsley, just once, be honest about how you feel.

"You look breathtaking in it," I offer.

Then, without waiting for her response, I push the curtain aside and retreat to my spot against the wall. I try to forget about the feel of her soft skin and the way she looks up at me with those ocean-blue eyes.

~

After lunch, the girls amble along until they reach a spot that catches the eye of Vincent's fiancée, Rosie. "Oh yes, let's stop here," she exclaims in front of a gelato shop.

Miss Slater lingers near the window, peering inside with a hint of longing. "I shouldn't..."

"What? Why?" Isabella chides her.

"Because weight gain is a career killer in my industry," she says, her fingers threading through her long auburn hair as she leans closer to scrutinize the flavors on display.

My jaw tightens. She's perfect in every conceivable way. I lower my shades to give her a piercing stare, and she glances in my direction, our eyes meeting for a moment, then she shrugs. "What the hell..."

Watching her choose a gelato is like watching an artist at work. It's utterly captivating, and I find myself pulled into the moment. I force myself to look away, knowing it's a dangerous game to get lost like this.

Out of the blue, a gelato cone enters my line of sight.

"Here you are," she says.

Immediately, my discipline kicks in. "No, thank you."

She frowns but does not relent. "Loosen up, Kingsley. We are in a small village. It's a hundred degrees, and I'm offering you an ice cream."

My days in the scorching heat of Somalia and Afghanistan flash before me, and only because it is hot as fuck, I ask, "What flavor is it?"

"Pistachio." She smirks, and I'm waiting for the other shoe to drop. " 'Cause you're a hard nut to crack."

A bark of laughter escapes me, and she stares at me. I guess it's a foreign sound, not only to her but to me as well.

"So we are checking out a few more shops down here," she says, and every minute counts.

I know we will cut it close to the engagement party if we continue shopping.

"One more, Miss Slater." I counter, eating the delicious nutty ice cream.

"I wasn't asking, Kingsley," she counters, striding ahead of me.

My frustration mounts with her audacity, a fire kindling inside me that's both irritating and invigorating.

It was like a strategic military operation maneuvering the girls back to the car, but we finally made it back to the hotel, and in time for their pamper sessions Rosie had organized.

While they're caught up in the world of hair and makeup, I take the opportunity to conduct a security sweep of Amore Restaurant, the venue for this evening's engagement party. That's when I spot a potential hole in the security on the rooftop. I swiftly coordinate with local security to neutralize the potential issue.

All in a day's work, but the sense of relief is short-lived. My thoughts drift back to her, making it clear that the real challenge tonight isn't just about physical security. It's also about guarding my own emotions.

Back at my villa, a black tux by designer Tom Ford is waiting for me, handpicked for tonight's party. Stepping into it, I can't help but appreciate the fit—damn, it's like wearing armor but way more stylish. I slick my hair and tighten the knot of my silver tie.

Looking sharp, Kingsley.

Walking to her villa, the dressing room memory is like a siren song, playing over and over. I knock, half dreading, half eager for what was next. She swings that door open and—*damn.* There she is, clad in a striking red ensemble that leaves nothing to the imagination, showcasing her curves as if she owns the room. And that wild auburn hair cascading around her adding to the intensity.

It's a test of willpower not to let my guard down. If I thought staying professional was hard before, it just became nearly impossible.

Suddenly, the scene from earlier, the zipper, the tension —it's all right back, front and center. All I want to do is step forward and tear the dress into two.

So much for masturbating in the shower to relieve the mounting tension.

Tonight, I need to keep a safe distance from her because upholding my professionalism is becoming one hell of a challenge.

8
VICTORIA

I f he shoots me that look one more time, I might just melt. There's this mix of danger and desire that's pushing me to walk ahead of him so I don't do something I might regret later. But damn, Kingsley in a tux? It's a sight that is doing things to me.

"I've conducted background checks on everyone on the guest list," Kingsley says, his strides matching mine as we approach the entrance to Amore Restaurant.

He's been practically silent since I swung that door open, and it infuriates me.

Why is he ignoring me like this?

I'm not usually one for petty thoughts or child-like behavior, but something about him throws me off balance, messing with my equilibrium. I want to demand his attention, not just as a professional but as—what, exactly? I can't even put it into words, but I want more of whatever electricity seemed to crackle in that dressing room.

"Don't you think that's a tad overkill? Especially since they're Vincent and Rosie's guests?" I ask.

"I wouldn't be doing my job if I weren't thorough, Miss Slater."

"Look, can you please just call me Viki or Victoria? Anything that doesn't make me sound like I'm about to break a hip," I shoot back, half jokingly.

Maybe it's not just Kingsley who's throwing me off balance. Earlier today, Lexy called me, all stressed about that article from my last Australian interview. Now, it's been picked up and syndicated worldwide. *Just great.*

Then there was last night's family dinner, which did nothing to ease the tension between us kids and Dad. And let's not even get started on the way my parents barely communicate or tolerate each other. It's a pattern I've recognized since I was younger when I caught on to my Dad's infidelities.

It's like life decided to throw every possible curveball at me all at once.

"No," he counters, shutting me down. "We're here," he adds.

I catch a hint of his cologne, taking a second to enjoy it. Then his hand reaches out opening the door, and there's this zap, this spark, from his touch.

When our eyes meet, his darken to a velvety mocha, as if diving into mine. The world falls away, leaving just the tension between us.

"Enjoy the party, Miss Slater. I'll remain close," he assures, seemingly unaware of the charged moment we just shared while he guides me up to the rooftop terrace.

I take in the setting with a smile. Festoon lights twinkle above the dance floor, and flowers seem to burst from every corner. Right away, I spot Rosie, the glowing fiancée, and my brother, Vincent, clearly enamored with each other as they mingle with guests.

Finally, a night where I can just be myself. I exhale a sigh of relief and start to move toward Rosie, only to be intercepted by a group of people I assume are Vincent's acquaintances that I haven't met yet. I sense my protector nearby, ever vigilant, as the group closes in around me. "It's okay." I signal to Kingsley with a sharp nod, reassuring him that I'm comfortable with the situation.

"Viki Slate! It's so nice to finally meet you. I'm Georgia," one of them exclaims, breaking the ice.

"Hi, Georgia," I reply, a bit surprised.

A woman beside her bursts forward, chiding, "Stop fangirling, Georgia."

"I love your music, Viki. Could I get a photo?" She doesn't wait for an answer and holds her camera up.

"Oh, sure," I say, somewhat taken aback. I didn't expect to be recognized tonight.

"So you've just been on tour," Georgia chimes in.

"Shh... don't bring that up," her friend interrupts, giving Georgia a not-so-subtle elbow.

"It's so nice you could take time out of your busy schedule for Vincent's engagement," Georgia continues.

"Well, he is my brother," I say, somewhat amused by their enthusiasm.

Both women giggle like schoolgirls, even though they must be in their fifties.

Just then, their presumed husbands join the conversation. "Viki Slate," one of them announces, eyeing me from head to toe. I feel a cringe coming on under his scrutinizing gaze. "Darius Floyd, from Byrnstrom," he adds.

As they bombard me with attention, I can't help but sense Kingsley lurking nearby, watchful as ever, and it's oddly comforting.

"Hello," I respond cautiously, then it clicks. "Byrnstrom? The latest acquisition from Slater Corp?"

"Indeed. Vincent invited me more as a gesture than anything else," he replies cryptically.

Unsure of his meaning, I just nod. "Oh darling, stop it. You're boring her," his wife interjects, her jewelry dripping with emeralds the size of rocks.

"Well, congratulations. If you'll excuse me, I must go congratulate my brother and Rosie," I say, eager to escape the awkward exchange.

"Okay, let's catch up later for a drink then?" one of the women calls out, craning her neck as I start to walk away.

"Sure thing." I smile in reply.

Kingsley smoothly moves ahead of me, efficiently clearing a path so I can extricate myself from the group. He quickly falls back into step beside me, his presence a reassuring constant. Up ahead, I spot Julius and Isabella alone at a bar table. Eager for some family in the midst of this social maze, I quicken my pace to greet them.

"Julius, Isabella! What are you both doing over here alone?"

"We like being alone," Julius offers when I envelop them both in a warm embrace.

As I step back, I bump into what feels like a brick wall, which I instantly recognize as Kingsley by his distinct scent. I'm about to stumble and fall flat on my face when I feel his large hands catch me by my arms, his fingers unintentionally grazing the underside of my breasts. Annoyance knits my brows, but an unfamiliar warmth spreads from deep within me.

"Shit, Kingsley, must you hover so close? It's just a party!" I scold, rolling my eyes.

Kingsley maintains a poker face. "It's my job, Miss

Slater," he responds in his deep baritone voice, his eyes zeroing into mine.

Ignoring the warmth of his gaze, I fold my arms and sigh. "See what I have to deal with?" I can feel my cheeks flush, but I try to shake it off.

Isabella and Julius laugh, seemingly amused by my annoyance.

"Keep it up, Kingsley." Julius gives him a knowing nod, and I shake my head.

Isabella is telling me about the time when Fox spilled ketchup all over Julius' rug, and my laughter is interrupted by two men approaching us, their matching grins as wide as their confident strides.

I immediately recognize them as both Vincent and Julius' long-term friends, Caleb and Harry, both harmless but shameless playboys.

"Oh God. Fabio one and two have arrived. That's my cue to get another drink," I say, spotting the men approaching.

"Who?" Isabella inquired

Julius lets out a chuckle, knowing exactly what I'm talking about.

"I'll tell you later. Bye!" I leave as does my shadow.

While listening to Vincent's speech, I sip my margarita, savoring the salt on the rim. I'm a bit buzzed, feeling lonelier than I'd like to admit, and yes, irrationally jealous. Both my strong, intimidating brothers have found love, and here I am, the perpetually single sister.

I draw a deep breath to steady myself. There are so many attractive people here, men and women alike. A few have even offered Kingsley drinks, but he's not touching any of them. He's on duty, which should comfort me, yet it doesn't. Because he won't even touch me. And it's been a long time since anyone has.

My romantic life has been a blur of fleeting encounters squeezed in between hectic schedules and tour dates. Nothing substantial, nothing like what my brothers have.

Vincent's speech draws to a close, and we all raise our glasses to toast the engaged couple. It's been a wonderful night, but I can't shake this low feeling that's settled over me.

As if sensing my desperation, Jasper Flynn—an associate of my brothers I've met at previous events—approaches me. I'm aware of his playboy reputation, but tonight, a distraction is exactly what I need.

"Aren't you a vision in red," he says predictably, but tonight, I'll take the compliment.

"Nice to see you again, Jasper," I reply, laying on the flirtation thick.

Beside me, I feel Kingsley go rigid, his gaze flickering over me before refocusing. I take Jasper's glass and down it quickly, feeling the bubbly prosecco lighten my mood as it slides down my throat.

"All these couples, it's such a travesty everyone's getting hitched, don't you think?" Jasper says, taking his empty glass and flagging down a waiter for another.

I laugh, grateful for the break in my internal monologue. "I couldn't agree more," I say, my eyes meeting Kingsley's for a moment before I turn back to Jasper.

Jasper hands me another glass, and I hear Kingsley clear his throat in that maddeningly disapproving way of his.

"Is that your bodyguard?" Jasper asks, tipping his head to the side.

I turn and lock eyes with Kingsley, who looks like he's on the verge of full-blown irritation. But really, who cares? I'm a grown woman, and I make my own choices.

"Yes, he is. And he's incredibly annoying," I quip, maintaining eye contact with Kingsley just long enough to see his expression tighten.

I turn back to Jasper, take the flute of bubbles, and down it in one smooth motion. His eyes widen, a mix of surprise and delight flashing across his face.

"Do you want to get out of here?" Jasper asks, the anticipation palpable.

My answer is immediate and infused with a renewed sense of freedom. "Yes."

The alcohol's foggy veil lifts just enough for reality to pierce through, and suddenly, I'm hyperaware of my surroundings. We're back at my villa, and Jasper is practically tearing my dress off as if it's on fire.

One minute, I wanted this, the attention and a break from the emotional strain, an escape from loneliness. But now that we're alone, and Kingsley's stabilizing presence is absent, the desire wanes. Fear rises, slithering over my skin like a snake, replacing the warmth of anticipation with cold regret.

As Jasper fumbles with the clasp of my strapless bra, I close my eyes for a moment, imagining it's Kingsley's touch. But the carelessness, the lack of a gentle touch, snaps me back to reality.

It's not Kingsley.

It's Jasper, and this isn't what I want.

"No," I manage to say, pushing against his bare chest to

create some space. My voice might be slurred, but my intentions are crystal clear. I need this to stop.

Right now.

"Shh... Viki, baby," he says, leans forward and puts his lips on mine in a wet, tongue-filled kiss that has me near nauseous.

I pull back. "Jasper, *no!*"

He looks at me, then down at my body, my red lingerie. "You don't mean that. You asked me back here. You will like it, I promise."

He pushes me back down on the bed, and his crushing weight falls upon me. My chest constricts while fear laces my throat, suffocating my voice.

No, I don't want this.

Images of the kidnapping come flooding in. When a hand touches me against my will, I find my voice again. It comes forward like a burst of stored energy, wanting to be released.

"Stop!" I scream out, but it's like he doesn't hear. Instead, he continues and starts to unzip his pants, so I bite his ear.

"Ah, fuck!" he says, and I taste the metallic tang of blood in my mouth.

The next thing I see is Kingsley's shadow standing beyond him. In one quick motion, he pulls him off me and against the wall, hitting him hard in the stomach.

"What the fuck!?" Jasper yells when he doubles over in pain.

Kingsley hits him again, and this time, I hear a crack from inside Jasper as he slides down the wall.

"Get the fuck up," Kingsley's voice is filled with malice and darkness, like nothing I've ever heard from him before.

"Stop!" I yell at him, not wanting him to kill Jasper but just wanting him the hell away from me.

Quickly, his gaze falls upon me, and it's pure rage behind his eyes.

"Kingsley, get him out of here," I beg.

His eyes immediately soften as he snaps out of his rage.

He yanks Jasper by the shirt, lifting him up and out of my room. My legs curl up as I hear Kingsley issue a menacing warning. Phrases like 'skin suit' and 'disappear if you ever touch her again' reach my ears, and it dawns on me that he's truly fearless.

Then he's back. I sense his presence before my eyes even meet his. When I open my eyes, a weight seems to lift, even if just a fraction. I swipe away a single tear, and it hits me—here I am, in lingerie, with Kingsley in my room. I should be embarrassed, but I'm not.

Without a word, he reaches for a robe and carefully drapes it over my shoulders. Assisting me into it, he ties the silk tie at my waist, and I find myself grateful for his presence and this gentlemanly gesture.

"Maybe I should ask if you're okay, but I'm so mad at you," he says slowly and cautiously.

"Could you be a little more considerate right now?" I say, but it's a weak jab.

He edges onto the foot of the bed. "You didn't want this tonight, yet you went through with it anyway."

"You don't know that," I object.

"I don't like brats, Victoria," he warns, his voice lowering to an octave that activates something inside me.

"You used my first name," I note, surprised.

His lips flatten into a smile. "Maybe it's time I did. I'm used to wome—" He stops short before correcting himself. "People obeying me," he says, gesturing between us.

The slip-up doesn't pass me by, and I'm curious but too tired to dig into it now. "Maybe it was a mistake to invite him back, but all I wanted was to feel connected to someone," I confess, lifting my eyes to meet his. I see a flicker of understanding cross his face, but I go on. "That doesn't give him the right to nearly force himself on me, especially after I said no."

"I agree, and he knows the consequences should he ever come near you again." His voice is menacingly low.

"Victoria, this isn't going to work if you don't listen to me," he says, his fingers toying with the end of my robe. A surge of heat flashes through me at his proximity.

"I will," I say, partly because I want him to keep me safe and partly because I like having him close.

Something unspoken swirls between us, a palpable tension that neither of us is ready to address. Still rattled from the encounter with Jasper, I choose safer ground. "Thank you for tonight," I say softly, looking into his eyes.

"No need to thank me, Miss Slater. It's the job," he says, letting go of the end of my robe.

I'm disappointed that he's back to formalities, but I lean back and slide into bed, utterly exhausted.

"Stay till I fall asleep?" I ask, even though I can feel myself already drifting off.

"Yes," he says after a moment's pause, and I hear him settle into the corner chair.

With that assurance, my eyelids grow heavy, and I finally allow myself to surrender to sleep, comforted by the knowledge that he's watching over me.

Kingsley has been unusually silent—even for him—since we returned to New York a few hours ago, and the quiet is getting under my skin. I find myself agitated and restless while he hovers near me in the garden. My mind keeps circling back to his earlier comment about being "used to women... people obeying him." It didn't come across as misogynistic, and I'm puzzled, trying to understand what he meant.

"Why won't you press charges?" he finally asks, his eyes ablaze and fixed on me as if he's about to explode.

That's why he's being moody?

"You don't get it. If I press charges, everything goes public," I say, trying to keep my voice even.

He clenches his jaw. "To hell with that. What if I hadn't made it in time? Did you even consider that?" His voice rises, tinged with a potent mix of anger and something else.

I straighten up, locking eyes with him. I don't appreciate his tone, but oddly, I find myself drawn to the intensity of his emotions.

Could it be that he actually cares about me?

My phone cuts through the tense silence, and I'm almost relieved for the interruption. Glancing at the screen, I see Rosie's name, which is strange because we just left one another on the tarmac.

"Are you refueling the jet to take me back to Sardinia?" I ask, walking away from Kingsley.

"Victoria," she starts, and the tone of her voice tells me something is very off.

"What is it, what's wrong?"

"It's Fox. Isabella's son is missing."

"What? Since when?"

"They got back from Italy, and she went to pick him up

from daycare, according to her agreement with her ex, and Fox wasn't there."

I feel a pit open up in my stomach. "Oh God," I mutter, imagining the sheer terror any mother would feel at that moment.

"The daycare staff said her ex, Travis, picked Fox up. He's not answering his phone, and the police have seen him heading north."

"He kidnapped him?" I feel my skin prickle with anxiety, memories of my own past experiences flooding back, threatening to suffocate me.

"Yes. I understand if you don't want to come, but—"

"Where are you?" I cut her off, urgency replacing any other emotion.

"We're just arrived at Julius' penthouse."

"I'm on my way." I hang up, turn around, and pin Kingsley with a stare. "Let's go."

9

KINGSLEY

It's been an intense week since we returned from Sardinia. Not only did I watch her sleep all night, feeling a peace I'd never known, but we were off again as soon as we got back to New York.

A frantic phone call alerted us that Isabella's son, Fox, had gone missing, kidnapped by his abusive father. We flew to Maine to bring him back.

Eventful is too mild a word for it. But Miss Slater handles it all like a seasoned pro, which makes me wonder.

How much did her own kidnapping screw her up? And how much is she relying on Valium to get through each day? How much is she tucking away, compartmentalizing just to keep moving forward?

She's strong, no doubt about it, but even the strongest have their breaking points.

I should know. I thought I was unbreakable once.

My mind takes me back to that fateful day...

"Western front's all clear," comes Carter's voice over the radio.

He's my best friend, a brother-in-arms, someone I've served with in Special Forces since graduating.

We're deep in the hills of a Somalian village. Our mission is to protect the locals from the local militia and secure a peace deal.

Twelve hours in, and no sign of the militia leaders we were supposed to negotiate with. They're late.

They're never late, and something's off.

Carter and Roger insist I go back to the truck to resupply and rest. We're running low on essentials. With a heavy sense of fore-boding, I make the dash. Stuffing my backpack full of ammuni-tion, medical supplies, and water, I'm nearly done when I hear it.

Gunfire.

The sound pierces the air, crisp and unmistakable. And then comes the radio's crackle.

"Enemy to the south, one hundred feet," Roger's voice cuts through the static.

In an instant, my pack is zipped and slung over my shoulder. I sprint back to the two miles to the hot zone, praying I'm not too late. Praying that the peace we sought isn't drowned out by the ringing of bullets and the loss of my brothers. But even as I run, the gunfire rings louder, and I can't shake the sinking feeling in my gut, the dread that says life as I know it is about to change forever.

"That was a great session, don't you think, Kingsley?" Victoria's voice cuts through my downward spiral when she emerges from the studio. Her face beaming from today's recording session.

Automatically, I fall into step beside her, and we exit the studio, I hold the front door open for her.

The LA sunlight cascades over her smooth skin, and there's no disputing her talent and beauty.

I nod, my gaze piercing hers before taking in our surroundings. There's always a tightness, a tension whenever I am with her. "You were good, as always," I say, my voice edged with a terseness I didn't mean to convey.

Victoria shot me a glance, sensing the undercurrents. "Kingsley—"

But her words are cut off by the screeching of tires. Every fiber in me is on high alert, and in a reflexive motion, I shove Victoria away from the road, away from potential harm.

She stumbles, catching herself with a hand on a lamppost. Looking up, her eyes, more worried than upset, met mine. "Jesus! You need to get a grip, Kingsley. That car was far away from us."

"I'm doing my job," I snap, but the anger wasn't truly directed at her.

I know I'm good at my job, yet I'm constantly doubting myself. Every little noise, every unexpected movement sends waves of anxiety.

"Your job is to protect me, not to kill me," Victoria replies, regains her composure, and walks ahead toward the black SUV.

I exhale and rake a hand through my hair. Each face that flashes in my mind is a ghost of a past I can't escape.

We return to her Los Angeles mansion on Alpine Drive, and I stand in the doorway seeking release. My hands are balled to my sides. Since starting with her, I'm bound tighter than a boa constrictor around prey.

You can see she's done very well for herself.

Her house is all marble and has expensive finishes. It's colorful. Too colorful for me. Her art is like a unicorn and rainbow babies, and I'm sure it's like a gazillion dollars. Again, it's not my style, not that I have one.

A luxurious lap pool extends to a yard surrounded by high trees. My accommodation is a studio nearest to the pool along the west wing. But with all glass hallways, I have a clear line of sight into the house.

It's private and gated, and after a few changes to her onsite security team and system, I'm content with the protocols we have in place.

"You can go," she says, dismissing me quickly and fetches herself a pitcher of lime and water.

"I'll be back at eight a.m. to drop you off," I announce, my voice tinged with irritation.

"Fine," she fires back, equally annoyed.

"Fine," I echo, barely audible, and my eyes drift to her midriff for a fleeting moment before I turn away.

I storm into the pool room, my fists aching for something to hit. There it is—the punching bag I set up this week. I don't bother gloving up. I slam my fist into it hard. Then again. The impact resonates through my arms but does nothing to douse the inferno within me. I pause, out of breath but not out of anger. I need some kind of release, and soon.

Making my way to the shower, I let the hot water wash over me in an attempt to cleanse my body, if not my emotions.

I towel off then change, my stomach grumbling. I find the con carne the chef left in the refrigerator. It's delicious, the flavors rich and layered, but even as I eat, I can't shake the tension that's gripping me.

It's then, I remember, the name Dante Blade.

Dante is the man behind the exclusive Vanilla Club chain. Special Forces veteran and entrepreneur, he'd given me an honorary membership after a visit to one of his clubs.

I'd been to the one in New York, but there was sure to be one on the West Coast.

The idea lights a spark in my mind. Dante's clubs are renowned for offering a sort of sanctuary, an escape from reality, and I realize this might be exactly the release I'm searching for.

This tension between us—it's a distraction, a danger. I can't protect her if I'm not at my best, mentally and emotionally. Tonight, I decide, is about blowing off steam and finding a way to cleanse this internal chaos.

I pull out my laptop, do a quick Google search, and locate a new club in West Hollywood.

The description reads private rooms specializing in BDSM and a main stage for live action and demonstrations. *Perfect*.

In under twenty minutes, I'm there. A huge arched doorway with security is the only giveaway to its location.

The security looks me up and down, and without anything to give him, I just give him my name.

"Kingsley Williams."

The guard speaks into his intercom. After a pause, he nods and swings the door open.

I step inside the dark room.

Let the fun begin.

IO
VICTORIA

The tension with Kingsley has me pacing the floor, too wired to even think about sleep. This back-and-forth we've been having is draining, and I can't take it anymore. Enough is enough. We need to talk this out.

With a sense of resolve, I head down the long foyer that leads to the pool wing where his suite is. I knock loud and clear, fully expecting to hear his voice. But there's nothing. Just silence on the other side of the door.

I decide to push the door open, and half expect him to be sleeping, but nope, as I walk around the room, I discover he's not home. And damn, his place is like a museum—everything's immaculate—folded clothes, shoes lined up like soldiers, and toiletries all in a row, neatly spaced. The faint steam in the air hints at a recent shower. There's a laptop open on a table, the only sign that someone's been around. I twist it my way, and there it is in bold.

Club Caramel by Dante West.

Surprise washes over me, but it's quickly overtaken by a buzz of excitement. Dante West's new mixed-sex club in

Hollywood? This has to be where Kingsley is. I've met Dante before at parties with Julius and Vincent. A quick scroll through my contacts confirms it—I do have his number.

Why is Kingsley at Dante's club? My stomach flutters, and my heart races. Well, there's only one way to find out.

Sneaking past front security is the hurdle. I rush back to my room, and a plan takes shape as the hot water pours over me in the shower. By the time I'm stepping into my little black dress, pulling on a blonde wig and strapping on my stiletto heels, I've got it all figured out.

The one hiccup is involving Lexy. Not ideal, but it's my only shot. With a deep breath, I pick up my phone and send her a quick text. Time to put this plan into action.

I sneak into the courtyard, where a security guard patrols the front gate, a precaution after what happened to me in Japan. The distant sounds of a honking horn signal Lexy's arrival. It's a straightforward plan, and it works. I watch while Carlos, who's on gate duty, leaves his post and heads toward the sound. Swiftly, I dart out, managing the best I can in heels, and open the gate to the waiting Uber.

I slide into the back seat with my disguise in place. Thankfully, the Uber driver doesn't recognize me, and I provide him with the address of the club, and he sets off.

It's at that moment I pull out my phone. I hadn't actually called Dante before, and I wondered if he would remember who I was. I think he would, but would he answer? Screw it, there's only one way to find out.

I dial the number, and after a single ring, a deep voice picks up. "Victoria Slater, or is it Viki Slate these days? What a pleasant surprise."

I'm relieved he remembers me. "Dante. Hi. How are you?"

"All the better now that I'm speaking with you." Ah,

that's right. The playboy flirt. The memories of our brief encounters linger from those moments before my brothers made it clear that I'm not someone to be trifled with.

"Still the flirt, I see." I chuckle, aware that his advances are all in good fun.

"Till I die. What can I do for you?"

"I'm moments away from your new club in West Hollywood."

"Well, I look forward to welcoming you."

"You're... here too?" The surprise is evident in my tone.

"Of course, it's a new club. I can't leave anything to chance."

"I see."

"Does Vincent know you're attending one of my clubs?" he asks curiously.

"No, and I believe discretion is what you pride yourself on."

"Hmm..." he mutters but doesn't elaborate.

"Dante, please."

"I'll see you soon." Then the line goes dead.

I pay the Uber just when the door swings open, and I look up and see Dante himself. Tall, stubble dotting his sharp jaw, and undeniably handsome, the kind who could easily sweep women off their feet.

"Welcome to Club Caramel," he greets and stretches out his hand, which I take.

He kisses me on the cheeks and guides me through the grand arched doorway and past security.

"I hardly recognized you," he remarks while he leads me down the dimly lit hallway.

"That's the point of a disguise," I reply.

"Have you been to one of my clubs before?" he asks, his gaze assessing my attire.

"No," I admit, suddenly feeling a bit out of my depth.

"A virgin... I like it," he remarks, earning an eye-roll and a chuckle from me.

"My clubs aren't for everyone, Victoria. And the fact that you're here alone..." He raises an intrigued eyebrow.

"I'm not alone. I'm with my bodyguard," I say. "He's already here."

"Who is that, exactly?" he stops before a large room at the end of the corridor.

"Kingsley Williams."

"Kingsley? He's a bodyguard now?" The surprise in his voice is hard to miss.

"Do you know him?"

"I make it a point to know all my members. Although it's getting harder while we expand."

I want to inquire further, but I can't. Anything I reveal to Dante might find its way back to my brothers, and I can't risk that.

"Take this," he says, handing me a beautiful diamond-encrusted mask. "Tonight it's masquerade themed, so everyone's in disguise," he informs me.

Perfect. That'll make it easier to blend in and possibly easier to find Kingsley without him recognizing me first. I take off my glasses and slip the mask on. The cold satin brushes against my skin as it settles over my eyes.

Dante guides me through the doorway into a room that's like an extravagant fusion of opulence and secrecy. Red hues dance across the walls, and low lights cast a soft glow on the plush furnishings. Leather-bound chairs, velvet drapes, and mysterious alcoves create an atmosphere both inviting and thrilling. People are everywhere. Men and women, some wearing sexy lingerie, others fully clothed like me.

He approaches the bar and asks for a scotch. "And a glass of Cristal for my guest."

Good idea. I might need a bit of liquid courage tonight as I take it all in.

He hands me the glass and clinks it with mine. "Be whoever you want to be here."

I want to say I'm not here for me, but instead, I smile and swallow the liquid.

As we stroll, he narrates the space, his voice dripping with a mix of charm and authority. "This is where our members gather, converse, and indulge in a bit of decadence," he explains, his hand gesturing casually to the various corners of the room. "Over there is our private lounge for those who seek a more intimate atmosphere, and this..." he continues, pausing dramatically in front of an intricately carved wooden door, "... is the heart of the club."

He pushes the door open to reveal a stunning room bathed in soft candlelight. It's darker than the main area. Intricate metalwork decorates the walls and an imposing array of apparatuses—a spanking bench, a St. Andrew's cross, and various other instruments.

There's a woman dressed in nothing but a lacy one-piece. She looks like some kind of teacher, donning a little riding crop and slapping it on her hand while she walks around the room of spectators.

I try to maintain my composure despite feeling my cheeks flush. Dante's eyes meet mine, and he raises an eyebrow knowingly. "It's a place for exploration, Victoria. Our members find freedom in expressing their desires here and in the several play suites next to this room."

I nod, absorbing his words even as my thoughts spin with a mixture of intrigue and intimidation.

A man approaches Dante and says something to him

discreetly. "I have something to attend to. Just call on me if you need anything," he says, kissing me on the cheek, taking my empty glass from me and handing me another. "Although something tells me you will be perfectly fine."

His words leave me puzzled like oil floating aimlessly in water. But I nod anyway, masking my confusion. "Thank you."

The dim lighting of Club Caramel wraps around me like a sultry embrace, creating shadows where fantasies can play. The whispers of other attendees become background noise when I focus on the elevated stage where a live Dominant and submissive demonstration unfolds.

An instructor, all sharp lines and dark leather, speaks with authority. "If you follow precautions, wax play can be one of the safest forms of edge play."

My eyes zero in on the submissive with her porcelain skin and fiery red hair. She's on her knees, Dominant overhead, dripping red wax on her skin. I watch her, noticing how her posture speaks volumes about her curiosity and willingness. She's not scared, not fearful, but excited and aroused.

As the wax drips onto her cleavage and her Dominant continues praising her, a warmth spreads through me. My heart races, and I find it hard to breathe. My string of wayward boyfriends—none of them have evoked this feeling inside me.

My pulse quickens, and a flush warms my cheeks as I continue to watch.

Then, my eyes wander, seeking something familiar. That's when I spot him—Kingsley. Even in this dimly lit space, he towers over most, a beacon impossible to miss. His gaze is fixed on the demonstration, dark eyes burning with an intensity I've never seen before, even through his mask. Clearly, he is at home here.

There's an electricity in the air, then as if sensing my gaze, our eyes lock, and I hold my breath. My heart hammers against my ribs, not from fear but from the thrill of discovery.

The instructor's voice slices through my reverie. "The submissive holds immense power in this dynamic. Trust, communication, mutual respect... these are the pillars."

I find myself nodding, lost in thought. The weight of this realization feels profound. I look back to find Kingsley's attention pinned back on the demonstration.

Applause filters throughout the room when it comes to a finish, and the crowd filters out to the bar and suites nearby. Immediately, I follow Kingsley while he strides ahead of me, then enters one of the play suites Dante spoke about.

With my heart in my throat, I walk inside.

There are around twenty people in here, some already in the throes of sex while others watch on. Various equipment lines the walls, such as the riding crops that were just demonstrated. Beside them are three wooden crosses where submissives are catering to their masters. I think that's what they call them.

Fuck, I can barely breathe. Giving complete power and control to a man during sex isn't something I ever thought I wanted until now.

"Hey, baby girl," an unfamiliar voice says, and I turn and smile, watching a man approach me in a blue mask with feathers.

"Do you want to play?" he asks, signaling to the many apparatuses in the room.

The buzz of the alcohol starts to settle in. "No, thank you," I say politely.

He steps a bit closer. "Is it your first time?" he asks, making me uncomfortable with the proximity.

I take a step back, reminding myself that everyone here has been vetted, and Dante has strict protocols. Still, I can't help but feel suffocated by this man.

"She's with me, aren't you, kitten?" I look past the man to find Kingsley staring at me, his eyes framed by a thick, velvet mask.

"Yes, Sir," I manage to say, my voice barely recognizable as my own, and the man grunts, making a swift exit. "Thank you," I admit to Kingsley.

He turns to me, eyes locked onto mine. "Kitten, I did that for me."

"Why?" I breathe out, caught between relief and curiosity.

Why, *Sir?*" I look up at him, my eyes searching for a clue in his.

"Because I want to see how that black dress looks against the cross," he replies.

My gaze shifts to the cross leaning against the wall, handcuffs dangling from its top.

Oh God.

My hand glides over its wooden frame, feeling the padded leather upholstery. This is all so new, yet strangely inviting.

Kingsley's steps close the distance between us, each one heavy with intent. The idea of being secured to a cross was never on my mind, but now, it's all I can think about.

"What next, Sir?" I ask, channeling the role of the submissive I'd seen in demonstrations.

He halts right in front of me, our eyes locking, the

tension palpable. "Before we begin, do you have a safe word?" His voice is deep and serious.

Shit, Is this actually happening?

I nod, finally finding my voice. "Phoenix," I say the first word that springs to mind.

He commits the word to memory, then continues, "Use it if you need to, and I will stop immediately."

Even in this brief exchange, the trust he establishes cements the unspoken agreement between us. He guides me to the cross with one firm hand on my back. His movements are sure, securing my wrists and ankles with a practiced ease.

His fingers trace a path from my wrists down to my arms, eliciting a shiver from me. With deliberate care, he lifts the hem of my dress, exposing the curve of my backside and my lace thong.

"I've seen you watching, waiting," he murmurs, his voice laced with a seductive promise. "Now, experience what you've been craving."

A sharp spank lands, the sting both surprising and exhilarating. Another follows. I'm hot with need and surprised to feel an orgasm building with each strike he lands. But even amidst the intensity, the safe word, our safeguard, hangs in the air.

I can't use it.

I don't want to use it.

I trust him completely.

Craving more, his palm glides over the tingling spot, and I close my eyes to savor the soft touch. The air is thick with his woody cologne, and my need skyrockets. All this, and he hasn't even kissed me.

The heady mix of pain and pleasure, dominance and

submission, has awakened a hunger I hadn't known was there.

His fingers, firm and unyielding, undo the restraints binding me. "You've been a good girl," he praises, his voice a low growl. "But I'm far from done with you."

The weight of his gaze, filled with dark promises, sends shivers down my spine. "Sir…" my voice trembles with anticipation, "… I want more, but somewhere… more private."

He stares down at me, and a smirk plays on his lips, clearly pleased with my suggestion.

Taking me by the wrist, he leads me to a door off to the side of the playroom. The door opens to reveal a smaller room, dimly lit and filled with an assortment of BDSM equipment. Everything from ropes to whips, chains to this bar-looking thing with two loops.

It's a new world I'm intrigued to be a part of, and strangely, I'm hooked.

As the door closes behind us, sealing off the outside world, he pushes me against it, his body pinning mine. "You want more?" he whispers, his breath hot against my neck, "Then you'll submit to me. Fully. Without reservations."

I nod, my heart hammering in my ears. "Yes, Sir."

His fingers tip my chin up, and his mouth crashes onto mine.

Hard.

Unyielding

Knee-buckling kiss that has me on the tips of my toes.

When his mouth leaves mine, I'm left with a head spin.

Holy Fuck. This man can kiss.

I can only imagine what he can do with his cock.

Kingsley moves with deliberate intent, guiding me to a

padded bench in the center of the room. He fastens leather cuffs around my wrists and ankles—soft yet firm. I'm secure but not restrained to discomfort. The balance is perfect.

Memories of my past kidnapping briefly surface, where I was bound, but those thoughts fade because, for some unknown reason, I have complete trust in Kingsley. The clasp clicks shut on the last wrist bind, and he lowers his lips to my ear. "You're mine tonight. Mine to command and mine to play with." His dominance has me weak at the knees.

I've known Kingsley for a matter of weeks, but this is a whole new side of him, one that clearly fits with everything I know about him.

My heart thuds loudly, the rhythm erratic yet intoxicating. Each touch of leather, each tug of a chain, is a testament to Kingsley's skill and experience. He rolls up my dress, gliding it past my thighs and thong so it sits just below my breasts.

He selects a leather-wrapped handle with multiple suede strands from the wall. The strands run over my exposed skin, a soft contrast to the sting I anticipate. "You've been so receptive, so open," he praises, his voice dripping with a mix of admiration and dominance. "But now, let's see how you handle this."

The first strike is softer than expected, a teasing caress across my stomach that sends tendrils of warmth cascading over my body. Each subsequent lash heads lower until he is striking me across my clit.

I let out a moan, my panties dampening with each strike he implores. And then, as abruptly as it began, he stops, leaving my body tingling and craving more.

Kingsley draws close, his fingers gently grazing my

reddened skin. "Beautiful," he murmurs, his breath warm against my ear. "You wear my marks well."

I can barely muster a response, lost in the sensations he's stirred within me. But as I take a shaky breath, I realize this isn't just about physical sensations. It's about trust, surrender, and the deep connection formed between a Dominant and a submissive.

"You're so wet, kitten." His fingers graze across my moist panties, running down the seam of my folds above my thong. "Tonight, all I need is for you to be my little fuck toy, someone to use for my own pleasure."

Oh God.

"Yes," I moan out, wanting nothing more.

"Good girl." I hear the unzipping of his pants and the tear of a foil packet. He positions himself above me, his breath on my cheek. "Yes, what?"

The weight of his body presses me into the leather beneath, and I feel his erection dig into my thigh.

"Yes, Sir."

With his free hand, he teasingly traces a path from my collarbone, between my breasts, and further down my stomach. The trail he leaves behind tingles with longing.

"Look at me," he orders, and I find myself lost in the depths of his eyes, a world of dark promises and intense desires.

Slowly, he enters me, stretching me completely. And just when I think he has no more to give, he inches in further. He lets out a guttural groan. "Fuck," he bites out. "Fucking perfect."

His hips move faster, rolling into me harder and faster.

I pull on my restraints.

Oh God, feels like heaven.

My body responds in kind, meeting him, matching his

rhythm, our connection deepening with every shared breath.

Kingsley's voice is a deep growl in my ear, words of praise and possession mingling together. "You're mine," he growls out fiercely.

I'm so close, and although sensing my orgasm is near, the grip on my bound wrists tightens while he moves with more urgency, fucking me harder and deeper. My pussy clenches him, and waves of pleasure begin to crest. He captures my lips in a searing kiss, swallowing my moans and gasps until I am panting for breath.

"Kingsley," I scream out as an earth-shattering orgasm crashes over me.

II

KINGSLEY

The sensation is overwhelming—her warmth, the rhythm of our movements, the intensity of the moment. And then, unmistakably, I hear it, my name escaping her lips in only a way she can say it. The realization crashes over me like a tidal wave. I'm dick-deep in Victoria Slater, my boss.

I'm trapped in a state of disbelief and carnal desire. The knowledge that she's beneath me, my boss, the woman I've sworn to protect, the woman who has made me burn with intense frustration, should make me pull away. But I'm too far gone. The tightening of muscles, the rush of blood—it's a train that can't be stopped.

My shock deepens, but my body has its own agenda. Despite the turmoil in my mind, I climax with a guttural grunt, the force of it almost painful in its intensity.

As the tremors fade, the room grows silent, save for our ragged breaths. The weight of our actions, the breach of trust, and the lines crossed all sink in. My heart thunders loudly in my chest, each beat echoing the question, *What the fuck have I done?*

I carefully extract myself and quickly loosen her binds. Then I turn my back, trying to gather my thoughts. My responsibilities, my professionalism all have been shattered in a moment of weakness.

"Why?" I finally ask, my voice hoarse while I zip up. "Why didn't you tell me?"

There's a pause, then I hear her soft reply. "I didn't think... but as things progressed... I lost control."

I close my eyes, taking a deep breath to calm my racing heart. "In my world, Victoria, trust is paramount, and control is everything. You knew who I was, and I was left in the dark."

She rises from the leather bench, pulling her dress back into place. The red marks still adorn her skin, and for a moment, memories surge—of my lips savoring the softness of her skin just moments ago. I try to push the thoughts aside, but they linger.

"Kingsley, I—"

"Don't," I interrupt sharply, the weight of betrayal heavy in my voice.

I put more distance between us. I need time to think, to process. Everything has changed. When all I want to do is shower her in aftercare, I'm left here confused and annoyed.

"You should've said something, given me the choice. I was blind, not recognizing you, but you? You were fully aware."

"I'm sorry." There's sincerity in her tone, her voice barely above a whisper.

I shake my head, anger still palpable. "Sorry isn't enough, Victoria. This changes everything."

Victoria's movements are frantic as she tries to put herself together, the elegance she'd worn earlier now replaced by clear panic. Fueled by a mix of anger and a need for clarity, I reach out and snatch her mask off. Her eyes are now laid bare, reflecting both shock and sorrow.

"Look at me," I command, my voice firm.

She hesitates, then finally meets my gaze. Those deep blue eyes I could get lost in are now filled with regret and fear. "Kingsley," she whispers. "Maybe this happened for a reason."

My stare remains unyielding. "No."

Her hands tremble as she smooths down her black dress, avoiding eye contact. "I know I messed up. I should have told you, But please, Kingsley..."

Closing the distance between us, I force her to look at me. "We're leaving. I'll take you home."

She blinks, surprised at my decision. "You will?"

"Yes," I reply tersely. "But not because I'm okay with what happened. We need to talk. In *private*."

Victoria nods, trying to keep her composure as we make our way out of the club. She gets caught up behind a throng of people, and immediately, I step back and claim her hand in mine. I ignore how effortlessly it slides into my callused hand and grips its way around mine.

In the fifteen-minute Uber ride to her place, she's silent, and I'm left to sift through the night's events. That petite vixen in the hall snagged my focus because she was a dead ringer for Victoria—same height, same frame. Honestly? I wanted her because she reminded me of my boss. Disciplining her felt damn good.

Realizing now it was actually Victoria under that mask and seeing her eagerness to submit? Goddamn. I'm completely and utterly ruined.

How can I protect her now I've fucked her?

She exits the car, leaving Carlos, the door guard, puzzled. "Miss Slater... how?"

I follow, locking eyes with Mike. "Send me the surveillance footage of the grounds."

Her breath huffs out in irritation. "Am I a prisoner in my own home now?" she retorts, striding toward the front entrance.

She creates more space between us, but my strides grow quicker, and I soon keep in step with her.

Opening the door, we step inside. "If you're going to lecture me again, Kingsley, you can just leave," she says, tossing her purse onto the table.

"This isn't right, Miss Slater," I say, rubbing my forehead in frustration.

With a wave of her hand, she dismisses my concern and removes her wig. "Miss Slater?" She whirls around, revealing her auburn hair pinned underneath. "I think we're past that now, don't you?" She quirks an eyebrow and kicks off her stilettos. "And have you always been a Dom?" she asks, her fingers working to unpin her hair, letting it cascade down her back.

I hover in the doorway, a mixture of anger and regret simmering within me. "For a while, yes," I admit.

She sits on the bed and faces me, eyes alight with curiosity. "Why?"

"Let's talk about you," I deflect, the conversation increasingly frustrating. "Was that your first time being a submissive?"

She runs a hand through her hair. "How'd I do?"

"It *was* your first time?"

"So, did I do all right then?" she presses.

"Victoria." I take my hand to my head.

"I sucked, didn't I? You're probably used to amaz..." She

can't even finish her sentence, looking down, and it's more than I can bear.

"You were spectacular," I say, half from habit but mostly because it's the truth.

Her face brightens into a smile, and she stands, turning her back to me. "Can you unzip me?"

"No."

"It's nothing you haven't seen before," she insists. "Come on. Can't we just let this go?"

I let out a deep exhalation, my legs moving me inside her room before my head has decided. She peers over her shoulder, her long lashes staring up at me.

I suck in a breath as my fingers feel the cool metal of her zipper. She sweeps her hair across the smoothness of her skin, and I ignore the urge to bite and suck at the fleshy parts of her.

She holds her breath as the zipper lowers, and when it dips to show the lace of her thong, I hover. It takes me a moment to realize what I'm doing before I take a step back. The temptation too fucking strong in front of me.

"I don't think I can let this go, Victoria. I should hand in my resignation tomorrow."

She whips around, holding her black dress across the line of her cleavage. She's mad, but so am I.

"What if I promise to never speak of it again? Will you stay then?" she asks, a tinge of fear coloring her voice.

"I don't know," I reply, my hand finding its way through my hair. The reality is there's still a looming threat against her. Her previous security detail was subpar at best. I know I'm the best person to protect her, but not if my emotions get in the way. After tonight, how could they not be involved?

"We are both adults. We gave into a feeling. I shouldn't

have betrayed your trust, and I'm so very sorry I did. But I'm not sorry I gave in to my needs. I've never experienced anything like that with another man before," she murmurs, her eyes downcast. "Not before my abduction and not since. I liked being your submissive, Kingsley. I can't apologize for that," she says softly, and fuck, my dick twinges hearing those words.

"But if it's a matter of losing you or you staying, I promise I won't ever mention it again. I need you. You are the best there is, Kingsley, and I know I put on a brave front, but..." she lets her voice wander off.

"But you're scared." I finish her sentence for her.

She nods, and my cold, iron heart squeezes at her vulnerability. I can't walk away now. If something happens to her, I'll never forgive myself. I started this gig to have a clean slate after the Special Forces. To keep my mind active since my forced retirement.

"On one condition," I reply, stepping closer to her and tipping her chin up to face me.

"Anything."

"You obey my orders. I don't like brats, Victoria." *Brats get punished,* I'd like to add, but choose not to.

She peers up at me, and a genuine smile peels onto her mouth. The mouth I claimed only hours earlier that tasted of cherries and sweet heaven. "You have a deal, Kingsley."

She extends her hand for a shake, and I grasp it, my callused hand enveloping her smaller one, giving her a firm shake. Her dress slips, exposing the lace of her bra. I quickly turn my back to regain my composure before meeting her bright blue eyes again.

"Good night, Victoria," I say and shut the door behind me.

I turn the shower on to searing hot and let it fall down

my body, washing away the night's events. The sponge, lathered and soapy, runs down tmy abs.

I fucked Victoria.

Victoria was my submissive. The image of her splayed across the cross, her dress cinched up around her waist, and her lace thong has my dick swollen with need. My hand skims past my torso and connects with my shaft, heat wrapping its way around my shoulder blades as the memory of flogging her loops in my mind like a wet dream. I lose the sponge and wrap my hard cock in my hand and begin to pump.

Hard.

Fast.

Vicious.

I fuck myself hard and fast, knowing this is the last time I will ever think of her that way again. I let out a grunt as I quickly climb to an orgasm. Bright blue eyes stare up at me from bended knee, and the image is enough to tip me over, losing my load down the drain.

Any promise of anything more going down with it.

Victoria. Miss Slater is my boss, and I'll never think of her as my submissive ever again.

The devil on my shoulder sniggers back at me.

Liar.

12

VICTORIA

I slept with my bodyguard.

My dominant, powerful protector.

My producer, Gene, stares at me like I've grown two heads. I am thoroughly distracted by the hulk of a man who's king-cock was inside me last night.

But it wasn't even the earth-shattering orgasms that I can't stop thinking about. It was his dominance over me and relinquishing my power to him. I felt liberated, unburdened from the constant decision-making that fills my day. But more than that, for the first time, I felt truly safe.

Safe with him.

Safe during sex.

It's a word I haven't used since my abduction. And since then, I haven't remotely been interested in intimacy with anyone else. The thought of a stranger violating me like that had me curling into a ball and removing sex from my repertoire altogether.

But now, just when I've tasted what a dominant relationship could be like, it's come to a grinding halt. All because I had to stop Kingsley from quitting on me.

I sing a note, but it comes out forced and a bit pitchy. I motion to stop, and at the same time, I see my producer, Gene, look up at me, a bit flustered.

"Yeah, let's break," I say, vocalizing what everyone else is too hesitant to mention.

"Lunch?" Lexy offers optimistically as I look between her and Gene through the glass pane separating the studio from the production suite.

"Yes," I reply, open the door, and step into the room, joining them.

In the distance, Kingsley is on his phone, standing with an air of authority. I quickly push away the vivid memory of him staring down at me, his eyes ablaze with need and dominance when I submitted to him on the cross.

"You okay?" Lexy pulls me out of my daydream, one that's been on repeat all day.

"Perfect, just short on sleep," I reply, glancing at my phone. I notice a missed call from Rosie and quickly send her a text saying I'll call her back later.

"What was going on last night? I was honking outside your place at eleven," she probes.

"I needed a break. It's been a hectic week of recording. I had to let my hair down."

"Why didn't you ask Kingsley to take you out instead of sneaking?"

"Pfft..." I huff, my eyes drifting over Kingsley's broad shoulders and jet-black hair.

Lexy follows my gaze. "Mr. Control Freak would've had kittens."

I chuckle at her choice of words but say nothing. I like how he'd called me 'kitten' last night. It's imprinted on my brain.

"I'll grab us some lunch," Lexy offers.

"I'm coming with," I reply.

"You are?"

"I need a change of atmosphere," I say, brushing past Kingsley and deliberately grazing his shirt sleeve.

Today, he's dressed more casually. His sleeves are rolled up, revealing the sexy ink on his forearms. And I find myself wondering about the rest of his tattoos—where they start and end. Okay, so my promise not to be a brat is in a bit of a gray area with moves like that. I hope he doesn't notice. But then again, sorry, not sorry.

"Kingsley, we're walking down Broadway to Fanucci's for lunch," Lexy announces.

"Is it imperative you go, Miss Slater?" he asks, reverting to formalities in front of others.

I turn abruptly and collide with his broad chest. His hand immediately curves around my exposed arms, holding me steady, and I suck in a breath, catching the scent of his woody cologne.

I look up at him and swallow. "I'd like to go if that's possible," I say softly, asking for his permission. His expression shifts from concern to pleasure.

There's something in his eyes I can't quite decode. "You may," he replies. His hands lower, granting me permission to proceed through the exit where Lexy waits. The heat from his touch lingers as I go.

Whoa.

Fuck. I don't know why, but I'm so turned on right now.

Another few weeks have passed, and I'm nearly halfway done with recording this new album. As promised, I've refrained from being a brat, but I've googled '*submissive*' and '*dominant*' more times than I'd like to admit.

I don't necessarily like all of it. For instance, I'm not one to walk around with a collar, being a slave to a master. I sincerely hope Kingsley isn't into that. But the idea of being showered with praise and being punished for my bratty behavior? Now, that's something that piques my interest.

Things between Kingsley and me have been professional. Too professional. But the underlying tension is always there, simmering. I know he can feel it too. It's the way he creates space between us after he realizes he's too close. Or the way he glances at my mouth when he thinks I'm not looking, only to blink and school his features as if nothing happened.

Lexy finishes briefing me on tomorrow's agenda, which is pretty much the same as it has been for the last few weeks, except for a phone interview with *Good Morning America* in the morning. "Right, if that's it, then I'll leave you to it," she says.

"Thanks, Lex," I reply, sinking into the sofa and waiting for my green tea to cool.

"Sure thing, hun. Goodbye, Kingsley," Lexy says, walking past him and out the front door.

"Goodbye, Lexy," he replies, and I'm slightly miffed that he still doesn't use my first name—not since that night, anyway—but he'll call Lexy and anyone else in our company by theirs.

I look up to find him in my living room. There's tension between us when no one else is around, and I push it aside, not letting it interfere with the great relationship we've built over the past few weeks.

"If there isn't anything else..." His deep voice trails off.

"I'm bored, Kingsley," I say, crossing my legs on the stone coffee table.

"I see."

"You do see. All I do is go from home to the recording studio and back again."

He nods in agreement.

"Will you take me out tonight?"

His eyes bore into mine. "I don't think that's—"

"Please?" I beg with a tone I didn't know I had until now, looking up at the hulking figure staring down at me.

He swallows hard, his Adam's apple bobbing up and down.

"I will be on my best behavior," I say, motioning a 'scout's honor' across my chest.

"That's *not* a scout's honor." He laughs, and it's the first time I think I've heard him make that sound.

"This is a scout's honor," he demonstrates the actual gesture, and I grin.

"Well, you catch my drift."

"Fine, but I'm choosing the restaurant," he says without waiting for a reply.

"Sure. I'm going to change," I say, standing.

"No, you're perfectly fine dressed like that," he says, and I don't think he even realizes that his authoritative tone does something to me.

"Yes, Sir," I reply, and he halts his motion to leave and spins back around, his eyes burning, and I stifle a giggle. "No, I didn't mean it—"

"Let's go." He deadpans.

The short drive is cloaked in silence. He picks a restaurant I've strangely never heard of. I lived here a long time and thought I knew all the restaurants in LA. He pulls in near Bel Air, and a valet parks the car. At least he called ahead in the car, so they're expecting us. I know the waitress recognizes me when she falls into an awkward silence. However, we're in a private booth, dimly lit, so the other patrons are leaving me be. It's a relaxed setting, and I find myself instantly at ease.

"Two steaks, medium rare, with a side of radicchio and vegetables," he orders for both of us.

I won't lie. I like that he takes the pressure off of scouring the menu, but I'd prefer something more hearty.

"Of course. Will that be all?" the waitress asks.

"Yes," he says, slamming the menu shut and handing it to her.

"Actually, no, I'd like a side of fries," I interject.

His nostrils flare in annoyance, but since we're not doing this dominant-submissive thing right now, I feel free to order what I like.

"Sure," the waitress says, making a note.

I watch the way her eyes travel over him, and I'm immediately jealous, but his eyes meet mine, effectively dismissing her. She moves on, and I can't help but ask, "Do you normally order for your submissives?" It's the first time I've broached the subject since that night, but I can't help myself.

He tilts his head to the side, considering my question.

"Okay, sorry, we shouldn't talk about it..." I let my voice trail off, and silence follows as if he's weighing my question.

"Yes, I would if I ever took them out on a date."

"But you've never dated any of them?"

"No, I don't like attachments."

"Makes sense, I guess, considering your Special Forces background. It must be hard to keep a relationship going when you're in such a dangerous line of work."

He nods, then leans forward, steepling his hands together. "And you, Victoria? Something tells me you like attachments."

A nervous laugh escapes my lips. Why does this feel so much like a date? "I've only ever had a string of boyfriends. Nothing serious."

"You didn't answer the question," he probes further while our meals are placed in front of us.

She sets down two steaks, greens, and fries, and I wait for the waitress to leave before replying. "Technically, you didn't ask a question," I point out.

He gives me a pointed stare. "Okay, okay," I say, picking up my fork and cutting into my steak, loving that it cuts like butter.

"I don't know, to be honest. I've been busy trying to forge a career for myself, so attachments come and go. Nothing has ever stuck. Or maybe it's me." I shrug my shoulders and pause, looking up at him. "Maybe I've just discovered another side of me worth exploring."

He presses his lips together, his jaw set tight at my admission. Tension swirls between us, only broken by the motion of his knife through his steak.

"Have you always wanted to be famous?" he asks.

"Famous, definitely not. But a musician, yes," I say, devouring the buttery steak piece by piece. I pick up my glass and drain it. I'm not sure if it's the richness of the sauce or my nerves that have me emptying the glass so quickly.

He frowns, watching me. "What is it?" I ask, noting his expression. I'm more curious than angry now.

"Alcohol and Valium on the plane. I'm noticing a trend here."

I shake my head, maintaining my composure. "It's really just a way to unwind, you know?"

"If that's all it is," he replies, eyes narrowing as if he's conducting some psychic lie detector test on me.

It's as if he could see right through me if I let him, so I put on my best poker face. I don't want to delve into the heavy stuff tonight—the pill-popping and drinking that escalated since my abduction.

Tonight, I want to know more about Kingsley and indulge in this incredible meal. "That's it," I say, doing the scout's honor motion again.

A fleeting laugh escapes his lips. "You're a quick learner, Miss Slater," he says, his voice a deep, velvety timber that triggers an involuntary response from my thighs. He tilts his head as if deciphering some unspoken language my body is mumbling. "One more," he decides, pouring me another glass of wine.

Something about the way he takes charge makes me feel both seen and attended to.

"Yes," I murmur, my voice coming out breathy and charged. "One more."

What's happening to me? Normally, I'd bristle at anyone setting limits for me, but tonight, I find it oddly comforting.

Changing the subject before my face turns entirely crimson, I ask, "Do you have any siblings, Kingsley?"

He looks up from his glass. "I have a younger sister, Indy. She lives with her boyfriend in Texas."

"Is that where you're from?"

"Originally, yes. But I enlisted as soon as I could and spent my entire adult life serving this great country. Until a few months ago..." His words trail off, a flicker of something —perhaps nostalgia or regret—passing over his face. But just like that, it's gone, as if sealed away in some hidden compartment.

"You left, why?" I dare ask, unable to stop myself.

He sets down his cutlery. "Because I didn't have anything left," he answers, and I believe him.

I don't want to pry further. I can sense the deep emotional wounds behind his words. He picks up his cutlery again, diverting his attention to his meal.

Switching gears, I bring up my family. "Well, you know I have two brothers, obviously."

"I do," he says, visibly relieved to move the conversation to safer ground.

"Rosie is wonderful, and I can't wait for her and Vincent to marry."

"And Julius? He's recently married to Isabella," Kingsley probes, a note of suspicion coloring his question.

"Yes, and you met Fox, her son. They've only been married a few months, but the best I can tell, it's going well," I say cautiously.

"Well enough to keep up appearances," Kingsley remarks, finishing off the last bit of his steak.

I'm taken aback. How could he possibly know it's a marriage of convenience? "How did you—"

He cuts me off. "I've trained in counterintelligence for nearly a decade. It's plain to see what the arrangement is, although I wonder if it's progressed further now?"

"Well, you're not just a pretty face then," I reply, slightly irked by his bluntness, but he must have picked up on the chemistry I did when they were in Sardinia.

A smug grin stretches across his face, but I know how to wipe it off quickly. "So, where can I find a Dom?" I throw the question at him like a curveball.

His fiery gaze locks onto mine, and the atmosphere around us seems to tighten. "What?"

"You heard me just fine, Kingsley," I reply, my voice a mix of defiance and genuine curiosity.

I'm venturing into uncharted waters, and if he isn't willing to be my Dom, I at least want him to steer me in the right direction.

He meets my gaze, eyes burning. "Why would you ask *me* that?" His heated look sweeps over me, sending a new wave of butterflies fluttering through my stomach.

"Because you've awakened something in me," I say. "Something I've been curious about since that night."

"No," he shoots back, signaling for the check.

"Wait, I haven't finished my fries yet."

"Your body is a temple, Victoria. You should treat it as it treats you," he says, a note of finality in his voice.

I laugh and pop a fistful of fries into my mouth just as the waitress arrives with the check. He hands her a black Amex without glancing at the total, and she processes the payment swiftly.

"See you next time," she says, handing back his card.

His eyes haven't left mine, and they're ablaze— a complicated mix of irritation and something else. Maybe I've crossed a boundary I promised not to, but a tiny part of me enjoys the thrill of pushing him too.

"This conversation is closed," he announces, pushing back his chair with a force that screeches against the oak floors. "We're leaving. *Now.*"

I quickly rise from my seat, my heart pounding, and follow him out of the restaurant. We get into the car, and with knuckles turning white from the tight grip on the steering wheel, he maneuvers through the streets of Bel Air with an intensity that has me gripping the edge of my seat.

He's angry, and not just a little. But why? Just because he won't claim me as his submissive doesn't mean I can't explore other options.

Yet he doesn't like that idea. Not one bit.

And I think I know why.

I'm being a bit of a brat, intentionally ruffling his feathers by asking a question I could find the answer to myself. Clearly, he's not a fan of brats. And yet, here we are, both of us unable to avoid this electric tension that seems to arc between us whenever we're alone.

He kills the engine and opens my car door, and even though he's not looking at me, I take his extended hand. "Thank you for dinner," I manage to say, but he's already striding ahead.

He goes through his usual routine of checking all the rooms for security, leaving me standing in the hallway, contemplating my next move.

"We're all good here," he finally announces, reappearing in the living room.

"I meant what I said, Kingsley. If you won't guide me, then I'll find a Dom myself," I challenge.

His jaw sets like carved stone, and he steps closer, so close I can feel the heat emanating from him. His hands slide down my face, cupping my chin to ensure I'm looking right into his eyes.

We lock gazes, a silent communication more potent than words. He leans down, his piercing eyes leveling me just like they did that night. And just when I think he might—

"Don't," he rasps, his voice trembling on the edge of restraint. He starts to reach out but stops himself, pulling his hand back as if he's just touched a hot stove. "Goodnight, Miss Slater."

I watch him retreat, his tall figure disappearing down the hallway toward his suite. "Goodnight, Kingsley," I whisper to myself.

I slowly undress, the cool fabric slipping from my skin as I prepare for the night. Finally, I slip beneath the covers, the sheets cool against my heated body and close my eyes.

I can't sleep, can barely breathe, and am suffocated by need. Maybe this could work with him. I mean, there's definitely chemistry and trust. We've established that. We also know he doesn't do relationships, and I just don't have time for one, so...

I get an idea and leap out of bed, flinging the covers off.

Let's test this control he's set.

As I look back on dinner with Victoria, I'm caught off guard by the unfamiliar emotions bubbling up. I'm a guy who thrives on control, but tonight, I genuinely enjoyed her company. When she laughed, her eyes full of mischief, I found myself laughing too. It's both surprising and a little unnerving.

But the warmth of the evening is now shadowed by a rising, turbulent desire. The thought of her with another Dominant? It lights a fire of anger in me that I can't explain. Imagining her lively eyes dulled in submission to someone else feels like a sharp jab in my gut.

Out of nowhere, my hands are balled into fists, clenched so hard my knuckles ache. Part of me wants to yell, to shatter something—anything—to release this whirlpool of jealousy and possessiveness. But the harshest reality?

She's not mine to claim.

That's the bitter truth I have to stomach.

Get a grip, Kingsley.

Just as I'm trying to reel in my runaway emotions, a knock echoes in the quiet space. My heart kicks up its pace.

Visits this late are unheard of. My first thought is that something must be wrong, but there's been no alert from the front guard. Yet, there's this glimmer of hope, impossible to ignore. *Could it be her?*

I toss the sheets aside in a rush, and another quick knock propels me toward the door.

I grip the door knob and pull it open with haste, unsure what awaits me on the other side. Victoria is standing in her black satin robe, looking up at me. Her gaze washes over my bare chest, slowly tracing the tattoos on my neck and the ink that decorates my chest and abs.

"Victoria, what are you doing out here?" When she doesn't answer, I open the door wider. "Come inside," I say, not wanting to leave her in my doorway in the middle of the night.

I gesture for her to come inside, and she does, sheepishly quiet. I'm unsure what to make of it, so I close the door, and when I turn, I'm shocked to see her on her knees with her face bowed.

My perfect submissive.

The sight before me is a direct challenge to every ounce of self-control I have cultivated over the years, and immediately, my dick swells with indescribable need.

She lifts her gaze, her eyes brimming with raw desire. Her eyes lock onto mine, searing with intensity. "Please," she murmurs, her voice thick with need.

"Victoria," I try to say, aiming for professionalism, but the words come out breathy and raspy.

"I'm here to please you, Sir."

Jesus fucking Christ.

Instinct is screaming for me to give in to the temptation she presents. Without breaking our intense eye contact, I step forward so her face is near level with my groin. The thought makes me even more aroused.

"Victoria," I say, my voice tinged with defeat and a recognition that I'm crossing a line I vowed never to cross.

It's a warning, one I hope she'll heed—get off her knees and run in the opposite direction. But she doesn't. Her tongue darts out, moistening her bottom lip, which is slick with saliva. The air grows thick and charged, marveling at the woman in front of me.

"You look beautiful on your knees, Victoria."

"Only for you, Sir." I tip her chin to face me, and she bites her bottom lip as if holding back.

"What is it you want, Victoria?" I ask, my voice barely above a whisper, hanging heavy in the air between us.

"I want to taste you, Sir."

Fuck.

The desire in her eyes has me painfully hard. *Who am I to deny her what she wants?*

We've shattered the barriers. There's no going back now. "Are you sure about this?" My voice comes out as a raspy murmur, every syllable laden with the gravity of what comes next. I need her affirmation, that quiet surrender that tells me she's all in because holding back is no longer an option for me.

"More than anything, Sir." She exhales, her gaze never wavering from mine.

I step closer, closing the distance. Our mingling scents create an intoxicating atmosphere, and it's almost too much. My fingers find her face, sinking into the luxurious strands of her auburn hair as I guide her nearer.

"Victoria," I rasp. "If we cross this line, there's no going back."

The air thickens between us. Victoria's eyes meet mine,

seeking silent permission as her fingertips graze the waist-band of my pants.

"Sir," she whispers, her voice laced with desire. "I've never been more certain of anything."

The room's energy surges, eroding the thin line of restraint that has kept me grounded. I groan loudly, my escalating need overtaking any reason anymore. Her movements, deliberate and fast, fill me with anticipation when she grabs my already thick cock. She teases my tip with her tongue and holy fuck.

Then, when her lips make contact, a wave of pleasure washes over me. Her touch is both gentle and assertive, taking all of me.

"Fuck me," I grit out the feeling of her lips around my cock, almost too much to take. Then she lets out a sweet moan. "Do you like eating my cock, kitten?"

She moans around my cock again and sucks harder in confirmation, making my eyes roll in the back of my head.

Christ.

She cradles my balls and clenches. I'm close, so close. *I want to come down her throat, to have her take everything I have to give.* The thought has me on the edge. My hands sink into her silky hair as I pull her back swiftly. She lifts her eyes to meet mine, jaw open and surprised.

"I want to come down your throat, kitten..."

"I want that very much, Sir." Her chest heaves with each rapid breath, eyes wild like her auburn hair.

"What's your safe word?"

"Phoenix."

"Use it if it gets to be too much. Now make that pretty jaw go slack."

"Yes, Sir." She opens her lips slightly and takes my cock between her fingers and inside her mouth.

I slowly rock my hips, slipping in and out of her warm mouth and feeling her tongue on the base of my cock. I move faster and harder and sink into her firefly hair.

Fuck this feeling. My eyes roll in the back of my head, relishing in it.

She gags, and I wait to hear her say the safe word, but it never comes. So I thrust into her again, my cock sliding deeper into the back of her throat.

Warm.

Hot.

Unbelievable.

She takes all of me like a good girl. With one more sharp, swift move, I come in a rush down the confines of her petite, warm mouth and let out a primal growl. I look down and see she's already swallowed and wiping her mouth with the back of her hand.

I drag my hands out of her hair and wipe the tears from her eyes. "Are you okay?" I ask, getting her up on her feet.

"Yes, Sir," she says.

"I never want to hurt you, Victoria, but I love_fucking your beautiful face and hearing you gag around my cock." I stroke her cheek tenderly.

She steps forward and kisses me with an intensity that has me tasting myself and feeling more emotionally involved than I should. I push her back gently and catch my breath.

"No topping from the bottom, Victoria. You know I don't like brats."

She looks to the side, then back up at me with defiance. "I think I might like punishments, Sir," she sasses with a smirk.

"Is that so?" I ask. She nods swiftly.

"On your knees, crawl to my bedroom." Her eyes widen to the challenge, but she doesn't say no. "Naked," I add.

A slight smile graces her lips, and I can tell she wants this. She wants to be the perfect submissive. Yet, I don't know why. I watch her peel off the satin robe, her erect nipples peeking through the satin of her camisole. Then she slips the top over her head, revealing perfect breasts with rosy pink nipples.

"And the shorts, kitten," I direct, watching her intently.

Relishing the challenge, she slides down her shorts, revealing a gorgeous cunt with a tiny strip of hair.

"Mmm... That's a good girl. Now on all fours, kitten."

She does exactly as I say and bends down, her ass pert, and sways side to side when she starts to crawl the short distance to my bedroom.

My dick comes to life again.

"Is this okay, Sir?" she asks seductively.

Fuck, she learns quickly.

"Fucking perfect," I praise, tilting my head and stalk her from behind. "When you arrive at the bed, climb up and lie on your back. I'm going to eat your pussy until you beg me to stop."

A gasp escapes her lips, breaking the silence as she follows my instructions.

I stride to the wardrobe and grab a tie, swiftly binding her hands together. Remembering the leg bar I packed at the last minute, I retrieve it from underneath the bed where I stashed it when I arrived. Her eyes widen at the sight.

First, I attach the leg bar to the bed, her curious, watchful gaze following my every movement. Then, with her hands and legs secured, she's at my mercy.

"I love the feeling of forcing your legs open." I move in, planting hungry kisses on her inner thighs, and she moans and writhes beneath me. "You look so fucking beautiful like that."

Her breathing quickens when my lips get closer to where she craves my touch the most. My tongue dances with purpose, swiping across her clit, then down her wet seam. She tastes better than I could have dreamed.

"You're so wet for me." Her soft moans turn into urgent gasps as her body responds to my every movement. I lose myself, flicking her clit with my tongue harder and faster. She arches her back, fingers tugging at the restraints as her need for release mounts. I devour her, exploring every inch of her with an unrelenting hunger.

She's teetering on the edge, on the brink of ecstasy. Just when she's about to break, I stop, relishing the desperation in her eyes.

"No topping from the bottom, kitten," I remind her.

She nods, realizing her mistake earlier when she kissed me. Her need is evident, a plea in her gaze. "Please," she whispers, her voice a mixture of desire and desperation.

With a wicked grin, I dive back in, tasting her delicious cunt and swiping my tongue over her clit in flicks of the tongue.

Harder faster.

She shatters as I push her over the edge, tugging hard on all four restraints in the throes of her release.

I unclasp the leg bar and quickly loosen the tie. A wave of raw authority surges through me. It's a primal call, an undeniable need to possess and reclaim her. I hastily grab a condom from my bedside drawer, sliding it over my aching arousal.

Guiding myself back into her warmth, my gaze falls on her auburn hair fanned out across the pillow. I ease the tip of myself inside her, savoring the moan that slips from her lips, then plunge fully into her, eager to feel her inner walls embrace me entirely. Her gasp, her subtle surrender...

A guttural growl erupts from me. Our bodies just click. Every thrust says it loud and clear—I'm in charge, and she's all in. She takes me like a good girl. It's like we're speaking the same language. No words needed.

Damn, she feels like Heaven.

Her nails digging into my skin, her legs wrapped around me, all a sign of her submission. It's just skin against skin, her gasps, and those moans, a roadmap telling me exactly where she is.

Our bodies collide, and with each move, I'm driving her head closer to the headboard and us closer to that peak, asserting my control with every single, commanding thrust. "Your orgasm belongs to me," I say, locking eyes with her.

She lets out another moan, and her tight pussy clamps down on my cock as she comes in a rush. Her eyes, her sounds, that grip on me, they send me over the edge.

With a deep, primal grunt, I let go, feeling every pulse.

14
VICTORIA

Holy shit, that just happened, and it was so much better than I thought it would be. He comes back, towel in hand, and starts to tenderly clean me up.

He presses soft, almost reverent kisses to my inner thighs as he does, and it's like two worlds colliding—the Dominant Kingsley blending seamlessly with this caring, almost gentle Kingsley. I'm trying to wrap my head around how the same man can wield both power and tenderness so effortlessly. But it's a mind fuck after being leveled with the most explosive orgasm I've ever experienced.

He vanishes again, and when he returns, he's holding my satin shorts and camisole. He's also dressed now, but only in low-slung gray sweats, leaving his upper body bare. My eyes travel over the ink decorating his arms, pecs, and up one side of his neck. Each tattoo tells a story I'm dying to know. And let's not even get started on his abs. I knew the man was fit, but I didn't know you could pack that many muscles into one torso.

Is that a ten-pack I'm staring at? Holy shit, it's like I'm in the presence of a Greek god.

This man *is* a god. A specimen of raw, sheer muscle. He's not just a weapon. He's *my* weapon.

"Put these on before I fuck you again, Victoria," he warns, and my eyes travel up to his as they burn into me.

I smile seductively but grab my clothes from him. I'm completely and utterly exhausted, and I sense he wants to talk about the little stunt I pulled as he sits on the edge of the bed.

"We've crossed so many lines," he says. "But seeing you on your knees..."

I put on my top and glide my shorts up, lifting my hips.

"I need this," I tell him, and he turns to face me.

"I believe you," he says. "And I need this too."

I smile. "Well, then..."

He turns. "There are rules if you want to be my submissive."

"I don't mind rules," I reply.

"Your safe word, for starters. If at any time you can't handle things, you must use that."

"Agreed. What else?"

"No one can know about this."

"Done. Next?"

"I need to know your limits, what you feel comfortable with, and what is a no-go zone."

"No-go zone?" I ask, quirking my brow.

"For example, a butt plug," he says, and I laugh, his eyes narrowing on me.

"But I've never had... you know," I say sheepishly.

"You will learn to love anal play."

I blush.

"That's enough for tonight. I will email you a list of things I want you to answer honestly," he says.

"Yes, Sir," I reply, noticing the glint in his eyes.

"You may call me Sir or Master when we play. And I will only call you kitten when I want to play. Do you understand?" he asks as I rise to my feet.

He towers over me and plants a long, searing kiss on my lips. Just when I think he wants me again, he pulls back.

"Goodnight, Victoria."

The act of showering felt like a blur, and getting dressed was an automatic process. I barely slept for about three hours, leaving me groggy and disoriented, going through my morning routine.

Eventually, I make my way to the studio, my mind still struggling to fully wake up and gain some kind of attention from Kingsley.

However, there is a noticeable difference in his demeanor compared to the previous night. The confident and dominant presence that I have been so in tune with my desires seems to have faded away. In its place is a more detached and professional version of him. Now, it feels like he isn't paying me any attention, and I'm growing more frustrated as the morning goes on, seeing him so distant.

I sit perched on a stool, headphones enveloping my ears as I sing into the microphone. The lyrics flow from my lips, but again, today, my concentration is shattered. Kingsley's distant demeanor occupies my thoughts, distracting me from the music I'm meant to be creating.

The lyrics I sang lost meaning as my mind replayed our

interactions, his shift from the passionate, dominant lover to the composed bodyguard.

Singing the final note, I hang up my headphones, and Gene speaks, "Time to refuel, ladies," he announces, signaling our lunch break.

As I mingle with the group over lunch, my eyes keep straying to Kingsley, who stands conspicuously apart from us. The fact that he chooses not to join us today irks me.

Sandwiches and salads lay forgotten as laughter and chit-chat fill the air, but his calculated distance is a harsh counterpoint to the closeness we've secretly shared. It's like he is deliberately ignoring me, and it's getting under my skin.

A new message notification on my phone screen pops up, and my heart kicks into high gear. It's from Kingsley. My fingers tremble slightly as I unlock my phone to read his words.

Kingsley: *Remove your panties for the afternoon session and hand them to me. You have three minutes...*

I let out an audible gasp. Hearing me, Gene swivels his head toward me. "Everything okay?" he asks.

I quickly put on a neutral expression. "Yes, it's nothing."

Shielding my phone from prying eyes, I tap out a quick reply.

Me: *Really?*

· · ·

When his piercing eyes lock onto mine, a fire ignites within me. He gives a subtle nod, sealing his command. My cheeks flush furiously while I make excuses, trying to slip away discreetly as possible.

I excuse myself, feeling a sudden rush of nerves and anticipation. My heart races as I hurriedly make my way to the bathroom, the door closing behind me with a soft click. The cool, tiled space provides a moment of solace, allowing me to gather my thoughts.

Glancing down at my outfit—a short skirt that adds a hint of daring to the situation—I can't help but smile at the thrill of his naughty request. It's as if his words linger in the air around me, sending shivers down my spine. With a quick, almost impatient motion, I slide my underwear down, bunching the delicate red lace thong into my hands.

Just as I'm about to catch my breath, a familiar chime echoes in the air—a message on my phone. Without needing to check, I know it's Kingsley.

Kingsley: *Sixty seconds, kitten.*

My pulse quickens, and I can practically feel my heart pounding in my chest.

A grin tugs at the corners of my mouth, too genuine to suppress. *So he was ignoring me but missing me just as much?* The thought fills me with a sense of anticipation and long-ing, a delicious mix I can't help but savor.

With a deep breath, I leave the bathroom and reenter the world beyond its walls. My eyes quickly scan the room, landing on Lexy, my ever-efficient assistant, engrossed in conversation with Gene and his team. There's a sense of satisfaction in knowing that our secret exchanges are just that—hidden beneath the layers of professionalism we both wear like a second skin.

My steps carry me toward Kingsley, his presence magnetic as always. He stands, leaning against the doorway, his gaze intense and captivating. The air between us seems to crackle with tension, a silent understanding passing between our locked eyes.

"Tick-tock, beautiful," he utters in a low, smoky tone that sends shivers down my spine.

Without hesitation, I reach into my jacket pocket and retrieve the little red number. Holding it out to him, our fingers brush in a fleeting touch that sends a jolt of electricity through my veins. His dark brown eyes remain locked on mine, ablaze with a mixture of desire and something deeper. I want to savor his touch, but know we could get caught at any moment.

He takes the thong from my outstretched hand, his touch lingering just a moment longer than necessary, and he slides my panties into his pants pocket.

His Adam's apple jumps in his throat, a sign that's impossible to ignore. It tells me he's as affected as I am, a signal that's both raw and heady.

"Good girl," he says, his voice a low rumble that courses through me.

"Thank you, Sir," I return, the words a soft promise.

"Now get back to work," he commands, and the finality in his voice stirs something deep within me.

Work is suddenly the furthest thing from my mind.

The moment Lexy leaves, I'm at my laptop, flicking through an overwhelming number of emails. But only one name catches my eye—Kingsley. My heart races as I click it open, anticipation tightening every muscle in my body.

I've been waiting for this all day, and now, finally, it's time to see what he's laid out for me.

Kingsley Williams
Date: August 3, 20:35
Subject: Rules of Engagement.

This document outlines the power exchange relationship between the Dominant and the submissive. It's binding only between the signed parties, entered voluntarily with mutual agreement. It guides the relationship to please the Dominant and enhance the submissive's growth. The contract spans one month, renewable.

Section I: The Dominant's Role
The Dominant ensures the submissive's safety, emotional well-being, and growth.
Responsibilities include proper treatment, discipline, care, and using the submissive as deemed appropriate.
The Dominant molds and shapes the submissive, encourages growth, and supports her.
Mental well-being is safeguarded by the Dominant.
Faithfulness, honesty, and openness are maintained.

Section II: The Submissive's Role
The submissive's purpose is to serve, obey, and please the Dominant.

Trust is paramount as she follows rules and guidelines set by the Dominant.

Sexual needs are addressed as per the Dominant's desire, with respect to boundaries.

Respect, care, and prompt communication are maintained.

The submissive will not exhibit any brattish behavior or will suffer a punishment.

Section III: Limits
Comment Yes / No / Curious?
Oral sex
Swallowing semen
Nipple clamps
Spanking
Flogging
Being blindfolded
Butt plugs
Gagging
Wax play
Bondage
Choking
Anal sex
Fisting
Suspension bondage
Whipping
Caning

A prompt reply is required.

Kind Regards,

Kingsley Williams.

My cheeks are on fire, a flush spreading from head to toe while I read through Kingsley's email.

I can't ignore the thrum of excitement between my legs. I quickly reply. I want more of this. There's no point delaying the inevitable. I go down the list of limits.

Oral sex? Hell yes.

Swallowing semen? Well, we've been there, and I'm obviously okay with that. Pleasing him seems to be all I want to do these days.

I cringe at nipple clamps, but spanking and flogging —fine.

Butt plugs and anal sex? Never done that, but I'm curious.

Gagging? Well, I've been there with his massive cock, and I can handle that.

Wax play and fisting? Jesus Christ. Hard no. *Is he into that?*

Bondage? If it's anything like what happened at the club on the cross, sign me up immediately. There's something about him tying me up, my relinquishing control to him, that has me all hot and bothered.

What the hell is suspension bondage? Okay, I'm curious.

I go through the rest of the email and then review it one last time before sending it back to him. I notice the time limit on the contract is one month, and I'm not sure how I feel about that, but it's renewable, so I agree.

Dear Sir,

I have read your form.
My limits are:

Wax play and fisting.
Whipping and Caning.
I'm curious about:
Choking
Nipple Clamps
Butt plugs and anal sex
Suspension bondage

Yes, to the rest. I look forward to whatever is next.

Your kitten

I check my other emails, but I'm not really focusing as I anxiously hit refresh and wait for a reply.

Does he want to play tonight? What if he doesn't like my limits list?

It's been an hour and no reply. I wonder if he's reevaluating this entire arrangement now.

I quickly pour myself a hot tea, twisting the lid of the honey and adding a dollop, praying there is an email from him when I return.

Nothing.

Goddammit.

After I shower, I hit the bed, but rest eludes me. Another night of tossing and turning takes its toll, and before I know it, the weekend rolls around.

Saturday's schedule is pretty light, just a talk show taping in LA.

I am staring at my reflection. My team has worked their magic, and they're waiting in the living room to put the final touches on my look. Then it's off with Kingsley. Just the thought of him escorting me—whether it's to some fancy event or just down the hallway—still sends thrills down my spine.

I enter the living room with a graceful stride, my gown swishing elegantly with every step. And there he is, Kingsley, leaning against the window with a look that's a mix of intensity and genuine fondness—all directed at me.

Damn, the way he looks at me is like nothing I've ever experienced. It's as if his gaze peels away all my layers, diving straight into the core of me. It's unsettling and addictive all at once.

"Good afternoon, Miss Slater," he greets as I approach.

Behind me, my skilled hair and makeup team follows, their craftsmanship evident in every detail of my appearance. Their subtle gasps and exchanged glances speak volumes about their admiration for the final result. Of course, Kingsley's presence doesn't go unnoticed either, and I catch the soft moan slipping from someone's lips in response to his irresistible magnetism.

"Afternoon, Kingsley," I respond as casually as I can muster, ignoring the heat scalding my neck.

His eyes zero in on me as I approach, and I feel a quick flutter in my chest.

"Victoria, this is magnificent!" Phoebe, my makeup artist, exclaims with enthusiasm, referring to my off-the-shoulder Valentino gown.

"Thank you," I reply, trying to sound confident, but I can feel a surge of nerves creeping in from out of nowhere.

"Ready, Miss Slater?" Kingsley asks.

Panic begins to rise, coming from nowhere. He watches me with a curious gaze, and I clear my throat. "I'll just need a minute."

Quickly, I excuse myself and rush back into my bedroom. I open the side drawer and down a valium without any water. Instantly, a sense of relief washes over me. Calmness swiftly replaces the fear that had briefly taken hold of me.

I return to find the girls and Lexy chatting with Kingsley, but it's evident that he's not fully engaged, his gaze flickering across to meet mine.

"Ready." I manage to muster a smile.

The girls air kiss me, and we exchange goodbyes.

The journey to the studio is short, and my driver, Willie, is focused up front. Lexy is here, going over the interview questions and show timings.

After a brief interview with the host, I'm scheduled to perform a new song from my upcoming album. Nerves begin to stir in my stomach once again, but I push them aside. This isn't the time for that.

Lexy is beside me, talking, but her words are a distant murmur. I stare blankly out the window and notice Kingsley tilting his head in my peripheral vision. He's trying to get my attention. His intense gaze locks onto mine with that look he gives when he's up for some mischief, and I'm immediately intrigued. He retrieves something from his pant pocket, and I have to really focus to see it as he shields it from Lexy.

Oh my God, are those my panties in his pocket?

I burst into laughter, and he quickly tucks them away, his face serious as stone.

"What's so funny?" Lexy asks, looking up from her notes, confused.

"Sorry, just remembered something from yesterday," I say, turning to face her.

Wait, has he been holding onto my panties this whole time?

Lexy looks at me, her face a mixture of puzzlement.

"Right then, if you say so." She must think I've lost my mind.

The production manager starts the countdown as we come back from the ad break, and so far, the interview's been a breeze. Maybe it's the Valium working its magic, but who cares.

Focus, Victoria, it's performance time.

"Go, Viki!" a voice from the audience yells, an oddly familiar voice, and it freezes me in my tracks.

The accent reminds me of one of my captors, and suddenly, I'm hyperventilating. Panic grips me, threatening to overwhelm me. I glance toward the wings of the stage and find Lexy looking back at me.

Then, the lights come on, and my heart clenches in my chest.

As the speaker introduces my next song, she points to the front, indicating it's time. The band gets ready, and my heart's grip tightens even more.

And there he is. Kingsley steps forward, standing right in front of me. Our eyes lock, and in that moment, it's like he's silently commanding me to follow his lead. A nod from him, and suddenly, a wave of relaxation washes over me, melting away the fear gripping me.

The microphone feels less like a vice in my hand as I turn to face the audience. Three cameras pinpoint me, and my mask of terror is replaced by the show woman in me.

The next thing I know, the final notes of the song are filling the air, and the studio erupts with applause. The host comes over, offering congratulations, and as grateful as I am for their praise, deep down, I know this is becoming an issue.

I understand this isn't the first time I've faced these out-of-control nerves and panic. There's a nagging feeling that I might need some help as this panic grips me.

"What the hell was that?" Lexy slams the car door shut, her frustration evident. Kingsley sits across from me, his silence unbroken since my performance. He hasn't spoken a word since ushering the autograph-seeking fans backstage out of my way and guiding me to the car.

"I don't know," I admit, my voice wavering. "I just froze."

Lexy's concerned gaze locks on me. "This isn't the first time, Viki."

Her phone rings, and she glances down at the screen. "Dammit, it's the label."

"Was it that obvious?" I mutter, my hands tugging at my hair in distress.

Lexy swiftly answers her phone, her voice formal. "Benjamin."

Head of my record label... shit, this can't be good.

A pause.

"She's okay," Lexy reassures him, but more silence follows.

I'm internally panicking, feeling like I need to pull myself together. I lift my eyes and find Kingsley's gaze fixed on me, his expression inscrutable.

"Yes, sir," Lexy speaks into the phone with an air of authority. "I'll let her know." She hangs up and directs her attention to me.

"What? What do you have to tell me now?" I ask, my frustration evident, my fake eyelashes irritating the tops of my eyelids.

She hesitates, swallowing before answering. "It's not good."

"He's not canceling the next tour, is he?"

"God, no," I scoff, hoping against hope that everything isn't crashing down. "They'd lose millions. Benjamin wants you to take some time off."

I laugh, but when Lexy's serious expression doesn't change, I know she's not joking.

"How long?" I ask, feeling the sting of tears threatening.No, I won't cry. I won't let it all fall apart. I've worked too hard for this.

"Until you're better. Maybe a week?" Lexy suggests, shrugging.

"A week isn't enough," Kingsley interjects unexpectedly, and I'm taken aback. I felt like he was in my corner.

"I don't think you're part of this discussion, Kingsley," Lexy retorts, her tone sharp.

I'm caught between them, unsure of what's happening.

Kingsley's gaze is firm when he stares at me, then he continues, ignoring Lexy's protest. "Miss Slater is experiencing trauma from her previous abduction."

My heart races as his words hit me. His imperceptibility catches me off guard. *How could he possibly understand that my fear stems from that?*

"What?" Lexy exclaims, her confusion apparent. "That was months ago."

"Post-traumatic stress doesn't just vanish," Kingsley asserts. "With my background and first-hand experiences, I should know."

The discussion swirls around me, and the dam breaks. I begin to crack under the pressure. The threat of losing everything I've worked so damn hard to achieve overwhelms me, and tears well up in my eyes. I lift my gaze to

Kingsley, and that's when I let the tears fall. I can't hold them back any longer.

"Viki," Lexy's voice is comforting while she pulls me close, and I let the tears flow freely.

The weight of it all, the pressure, it's finally releasing. When I manage to open my eyes again, I catch Kingsley watching me. A pain in his eyes strikes me in the chest, but he makes no move to comfort me when I need it most. Instead, he quickly averts his gaze, staring out the window.

All I want is to bury myself in his embrace, but that's not an option. Not here, not in front of Lexy.

"How about your place in the Hamptons?" Lexy asks.

15

KINGSLEY

It's been just twenty-four hours since we arrived, and I've kept away from her, giving her space. We're in the Hamptons, a place I should have visited back when my best friend, Carter, died in my arms in the East Somalian Hills. It's where his child he never met and his wife still live.

I push the memories aside, a crashing noise from the living room catching my attention. Rushing in, I see her on the floor, picking up a shattered plate she dropped.

"You don't have to," she says as I come over to help.

"I know I don't," I reply.

Victoria just looks at me. She's been quiet since yesterday, ever since her emotions overwhelmed her in the black suburban after her performance. The fear in her eyes when she froze on stage, then leveled me with a stare from the stage—I just knew I had to do something. I had to help her through it. And when she pulled through, I was so proud of her. So damn proud.

"You must think I'm childish and silly for how I acted yesterday," she finally states, no longer looking at me.

Is she actually serious? I stop what I'm doing and lift her up. She's so light, too light.

"Get over here," I say and plunk her down on the island countertop, settling between her thighs and forcing her to look at me.

"I was so fucking proud of you yesterday for pulling through and coming out on the other side."

She looks at me incredulously, as if I have two heads. "But I froze. Everyone saw it. I can't bear to look at the media headlines again," she says, turning away from my gaze.

I grip her chin and angle it, ensuring she has no choice but to meet my gaze. From this level, we're face to face, and I stare into her beautiful, big blue eyes.

Her pain speaks to me. It's like a voice I've squashed inside of me too.

"Don't look. Focus on you. You have your first appointment with the psychologist tomorrow," I tell her.

She shakes her head, and it drives me crazy the way she thinks so lowly of herself.

I grip her chin tighter. "You will start running every morning with me, Victoria," I say, my voice an octave lower.

I feel her body shift in front of me.

"Was that in the arrangement, Sir? If so, I think I missed that part."

"It wasn't, but it's new and necessary for your mental clarity."

"And what if I don't want to, Sir?" she asks, biting her lower lip.

Is she trying to be bratty just to get punished?

"You know what happens if you disobey me."

"Remind me, Sir?" she pushes, a glint in her eyes that makes me twitch with anticipation.

"You can have my cock for breakfast, lunch, and dinner," I snap, pulling her closer to inhale her scent.

"I think I'd like that, Sir," she replies, running her tongue over her lips.

I can't maintain this distance any longer. I close the gap between us, wrap my hand around the nape of her neck, and devour her mouth with a kiss. She responds by pressing her body against mine, and God, I have to pull away. This is too intimate. I normally don't kiss any of my subs, but with her...

She looks back at me, fire in her eyes that ignites something within, pushing back the darkness.

I grab the kitchen towel from the oven and step between her parted thighs, widening them further. Then I seize her wrists and tightly tie them together, securing the knot. She utters a soft "ouch," and I trail my hands down her exposed arms, eliciting a shiver from her as I lower her back onto the cold marble surface of the kitchen island. With her hands above her head, I take a moment to admire the goddess sprawled before me.

She releases a small gasp when her back makes contact with the chilly surface. Our eyes meet, windows to our souls, and I reach down, pulling her thighs closer to me. The cold edge of the island contrasts with the simmering heat between us. I plant my hands on either side of her, effectively caging her in. "You like being a brat, don't you?" I inquire, reaching for a drawer beside my leg and pulling out a plastic spatula—perfect for what I have in mind.

"No, Sir," she retorts.

I give her thigh a swift strike with the spatula, eliciting a gasp. "Don't lie," I warn, landing another hit, this time on the inside of her thigh.

I lift the hem of her dress, and she arches her hips off

the countertop. "Mmm, beautiful," I murmur, marveling at her choice of a pink thong as I caress her folds.

Leaning down, I graze my teeth roughly over her clit, circling it through the lace of her underwear. Her groan electrifies me. I treat her to a few more strokes of my tongue before replacing it with a soft tap of the spatula against her clit.

"Oh God," she moans out.

I strike her again, and she gasps. "You dirty little kitten, you like it, don't you?"

"Yes, Sir," she whispers.

"Do you want more?" I ask, utterly captivated by the goddess beneath me, her soft, auburn hair cascading over her shoulders.

I'm barely holding it together. Her taste on my tongue has stirred something inside me I can't quite name. She nods, and that's all the confirmation I need.

I land two more strikes across her clit, dragging the spatula down her drenched panties, and press its tip inside her. Her loud moan fills the room, and the sounds coming from her ignite my already overwhelming desire.

The kitchen utensil clatters on the countertop as I sweep her into my arms. She squeals as I effortlessly carry her across the mansion to my room on the opposite end of hers. I navigate the hallways, each step taking us farther from her side of the mansion and closer to my sanctuary. I sense her gaze fall upon me and momentarily look down at her. Delicate and beautiful.

When we arrive, I gently set her down on the edge of the bed, my gaze locking onto hers. Slowly, deliberately, I begin unbuttoning my shirt, my eyes never leaving hers. "Remove your clothes, kitten," I command, and she follows suit, her fingers deftly unfastening the clasps of her dress. The fabric falls away, pooling around her like a fallen halo.

"Good girl. Now crawl up the bed on all fours until your head is near the headboard."

"Yes, Sir," she says, embodying the perfect submissive.

I lose my pants, watching her intently and staring at her ass in the air, groaning at the sight. "So damn beautiful."

Reaching for my bedside drawer, I pull out a recent delivery. After memorizing her limits and what she's curious about, I've selected some restraints, a vibrator, and a small butt plug.

She peers over her shoulder. "When did you get those, Sir?"

"Yesterday," I say. "Face forward. What's your safe word?"

"Phoenix, Sir," she responds.

I decide to warm her up first and switch on the vibrator, the buzz filling the room. Positioning myself behind her, I drag it up her thigh until it reaches her moist slit. I ease the tip inside, then plunge it in without warning. She takes it like a good girl as I move it in and out.

She moans.

"Don't come," I instruct and continue to tease her.

I spread her wetness up to her delicious ass, and she tenses.

"Curious?" I ask, recalling her limits list and what she's indicated she wants to try. I trace the tip around her back entrance, and although she's tense, she lets out a strangled sound. "Do you want more, kitten?" I ask, eager for her to experience this with me.

She nods, and that's everything I need.

"On your back," I instruct, turning off the vibrator. She's panting, full of need, and complies.

Quickly, I secure her wrists and ankles to each bedpost, aware of her eyes following my every move. Unable to resist her any longer, I lower myself for a passionate kiss, then trail my mouth to her nipples, taking each one roughly between my lips. My hand descends to her clit, and her hips buckle at my touch. I love how responsive she is to me.

"Tell me if it gets too much," I caution, positioning myself between her thighs. I widen her legs, leaving her beautifully spread-eagle before me, then switch the vibrator back on and hover it over her clit. Simultaneously, I uncap the lubricant and coat the tip of the butt plug.

Between moans, she glances up at me cautiously. "Is that going in my—"

"Yes, kitten. And you will take it like a good girl," I assure her.

Her eyes widen as I gently slide the tip into her. I watch her body embrace the surprising sensation.

"Oh God," she moans out.

"You will come only when I tell you to," I remind her.

I push the plug in deeper as she arches off the bed, the vibrator still humming on her clit. Jealous of the machine, I turn it off and delve into her with my mouth, eager to taste her and elicit this orgasm from her. She moans and writhes while my other hand pushes the plug all the way in.

"Fuck," she screams out. "Sir, please..." she begs as I stroke her clit with the flat of my tongue.

"Such a good girl," I praise. "Come for me, kitten. I want to taste you on my tongue."

Without waiting for a reply, I lavish her with rapid flicks of my tongue until she explodes into a quivering orgasm.

I reach for a condom from the bedside drawer and roll it on with practiced ease. "I'm going to fuck you hard now, so you're full in both holes," I announce, a smoldering intensity in my eyes.

She nods, her breath coming in short, uneven bursts, signaling her anticipation. My hands find her hips, and I position myself at her entrance, the tip of my erection pressing against her.

"Do you trust me, kitten?" I ask, locking eyes with her.

Her nod is almost imperceptible, but it's all the consent I need. In one smooth, powerful motion, I sink into her hard. She gasps, a sound of pure pleasure mixed with a tinge of surprise, and I stifle my own groan at how incredibly tight and warm she is.

With every thrust, I drive into her deeper, my gaze never leaving her face. I want to see every flicker of emotion, every flash of pleasure or pain. Her eyes are half lidded, almost glazed over, her mouth a soft 'O' as she struggles to take me in.

"You're so damn tight," I grunt out, my own pleasure escalating with each stroke.

Unable to resist any longer, I reach for the vibrator that lies forgotten beside us. I flick it back to life and press it against her clit. Her back arches off the bed, a muffled scream escaping her lips as she's filled with sensation from both ends.

"I said you'd come when I told you to, and I meant it," I growl out, leaning down to capture her mouth in a punishing kiss. My thrusts become more erratic, my pace quickening.

The room is filled with the sounds of our labored breathing and the wet, rhythmic slap of skin against skin. We're both close. I can feel it. Her inner muscles tighten around me, and I know she's on the edge.

"Look at me, kitten," I command, our eyes meeting as I feel my own climax building.

Her eyes snap to mine, filled with a mixture of desire and vulnerability that strikes me to my core.

"Now," I say, giving her permission.

Her body convulses beneath me, her walls clamping down when she reaches her peak. The sensation triggers my own climax, and I come with a guttural growl, my body shuddering above hers.

Exhausted, I pull out carefully, disposing the condom and releasing her from her restraints. I lie beside her, pulling her into the curve of my arm.

"You were incredible, kitten," I murmur, my lips grazing her hair.

The post-coital haze wraps around me like a comfortable blanket, but I fight the urge to sink into it. I carefully push myself off the bed and grab a towel to clean her up. While I tenderly wipe her, she watches me. Her eyes are soft, glowing with that look that makes me feel like I've been branded, marked by something indescribable. It scares me.

"Will you stay with me tonight?" Her question hangs in the air, innocent yet weighted, pulling at something deep inside me that I've kept locked away.

It takes everything in me to say the words that form in my mind. "I can't," I reply, my voice colder than I intended.

Her eyes, those deep wells of emotion, flicker with something that looks like disappointment or maybe understanding. I can't tell which.

The weight of my words fills the room, thickening the air between us like an invisible wall. Victoria looks as though she might challenge me for a second, but then her gaze softens, and she lies back against the pillow.

"Okay," she whispers.

That one simple yet heavy word recognizes the emotional chasm between us yet somehow makes it a little more bearable.

I lean in, my lips gently meeting her forehead in a soft kiss. "You should go," I murmur, even though every fiber of my being screams for her to stay.

She nods, her eyes holding mine for a lingering moment before she starts gathering her things. Stepping out of my sanctuary, I can't help but feel that each step she takes away from me pulls at something deep within me—something I don't yet understand.

16
VICTORIA

W hoa, kill me now.

The butt? Seriously?

There aren't enough expletives in the world to describe the orgasm that just shattered me from the inside out, nearly ripping me in two. It's like every nerve ending decided to host its own fireworks show, and I was the audience, the main event rolling into one.

But from an extreme high came an extreme low.

When I asked him if we could stay together tonight, he turned me down. I should have known better. This is an arrangement, after all. He's here protecting me. I'm his submissive. I am also meant to be sorting myself out, getting the help I need to overcome this overwhelming anxiety gripping me like a glove.

As I drift into sleep, I can't shake the way his eyes seem to pierce my soul, as if he's truly seeing me for the first time.

Kingsley is a man of few words and even fewer emotions, yet I sense something more—something he's fighting hard to suppress.

Should I do the same? Can anything good ever come between us?

My thoughts wander to the possibilities of happy endings. A sense of warmth envelops me, and finally, my eyelids grow heavy as I surrender to the darkness.

A stern knock on my door jerks me awake.

What the hell? What time is it?

Struggling to open my eyes, I realize it's still dark outside.

"Victoria." Kingsley's voice slices through the door.

"For God's sake, stop knocking and come in," I reply, yanking off my sleep mask and sitting upright. The alarm clock taunts me, flashing five thirty a.m.

"Running time," he announces, looking like he's stepped straight out of a Nike ad.

"Now?" I ask, scratching my head.

His gaze softens me a bit. "Now, kitten," he says, his voice dropping to an authoritative tone that weakens my knees.

Groaning, I throw off the quilt. His eyes drift to my satin camisole and shorts, and I feel my nipples harden. So, I intentionally lift off my camisole, putting on a little show.

He stands still, watching me like a predator.

"Like what you see, Sir?" I tease.

"Very much so, kitten. You know how to please me," he replies, his gaze flickering to my bare skin. "But if you don't get changed now, we won't be leaving this bedroom, I promise you."

"Can't I get exercise another way, Sir?" I quip, flipping

my long auburn hair to one side, knowing it drives him wild.

His eyes darken, heat thickening the air between us. "Oh, you will. You'll have me for breakfast."

I swallow, his words sending a rush of heat through me. "Something to look forward to, Sir," I say, quickly grabbing some activewear I have stashed. I see him smile before leaving my room.

Slipping into shorts and a T-shirt, I find him waiting in the living room. "I can't say I'm looking forward to this," I admit, already missing the warmth of my bed.

He laughs. "I don't love it either, but running clears the mind. It creates space. Helps you heal," he says, his eyes taking on a contemplative look.

It makes me wonder just how damaged he is. He's only given me the bare minimum about his life in the Special Forces. That sort of thing has to affect a person's mental state.

"Shall we?" he asks, stepping forward and opening the door for me.

~

God, the man is like Usain Bolt. Here I am, spluttering and practically coughing up a lung I didn't even know was full until now. We return from our run, and he opens the door effortlessly, a neat 'V' of sweat darkening his blue crew-neck T-shirt.

Next to him, I must look like a mess—red-faced, with flyaway hair all over the place, and probably smelling less than fresh. He hands me a water bottle, and I snatch it, gulping it down like I've just crossed the Sahara.

He watches me, and I feel a twinge of embarrassment. "Okay, so I'm out of shape," I admit.

He quirks an eyebrow. "Nothing you can't improve on. Every day's a new start."

"Oh God, don't go all Tony Robbins on me," I say, and he laughs, the sound making my insides flutter.

He looks pleasantly surprised that he's laughing too. "I wouldn't dare," he says, taking a hefty gulp from his water bottle.

My eyes are drawn to the way his Adam's apple bobs and the sheen of sweat on his tattooed arm. I step closer, trailing my hand up his arm. "I like these," I say. "What do they signify?"

He takes a deep breath as if weighing whether to answer. "They're birds... owls, an eagle, and a phoenix in the desert."

"Phoenix?" My interest piques. What a coincidence. That's my safe word.

"Yes," he nods. "They're tributes to my closest mates, my fallen soldiers, Carter, Roger, Toby, and Joel. The phoenix represents my best friend, Carter. He died in my arms, but I like to think of him as immortal." He looks surprised that he told me that, but I'm so grateful to him for sharing something so personal with me.

"I'm so sorry," I say, feeling my eyes well up. "Will you tell me what happened?" I ask softly, his arm resting against my cheek, his fingers gently tucking a stray strand of hair behind my ear.

"One day, but right now, you have to get ready for Dr. Diedra."

Ugh, my therapist. I can't tell if he's avoiding the topic or genuinely planning to share later. Time will tell.

My fingers lightly brush over the Phoenix tattoo, and he shivers slightly. Then he plants a kiss on my forehead. "I'm going to take a shower, then drive you to Montauk," he says.

"Do you eat?" I ask, still reveling in the warmth of his touch.

"All the time," he says, his eyes sparkling, the atmosphere shifting.

I blush, feeling a pang of jealousy at the thought that he's likely had a string of submissives before me. The idea of him with another woman sends a shiver down my spine that's part envy, part arousal. "How about breakfast after we see Dr. Diedra?"

His smile is my undoing. It liquefies my bones, making me weak. "I was thinking the same," he replies. But now, with that smile, I don't think I can wait.

I follow him, every step widening the physical gap but doing nothing to lessen my emotional craving for him. He pivots suddenly, locking eyes with me, and the air between us crackles with tension. "Sir, I need my breakfast now," I assert, my voice tinged with longing and desire.

"Goddamn," he mutters, tipping my chin up to meet his eyes. "What are you doing to me, Victoria?" His mouth finds mine, and he kisses me with an intensity that could blow my kneecaps out if he weren't holding me upright. Without another word, he grabs my hand, practically dragging me toward his ensuite.

～

As I walk into the office, I'm immediately struck by the warm ambiance. I've talked to Dr. Diedra on the phone before. She's the best in the business, hired by my record label to help me navigate this rough patch. But being here in person feels different, more intimate, and that makes me nervous.

"How are you today?" Dr. Diedra asks, her eyes meeting mine as she sits.

"Anxious," I reply, choosing my words carefully.

"Do you want to delve into what's causing this anxiety?" she asks, pen poised over her notebook.

I hesitate. Sure, she's reputable, even recommended by people I trust at the label. But trust doesn't come easily to me, thanks to a childhood colored by my father's infidelities. "I'm ready to talk about... the kidnapping," I manage to say, avoiding eye contact.

Dr. Diedra puts her pen down, leaning forward. "Take all the time you need. You're safe here."

I opt for the bare details, cautiously skimming the surface of the emotional depth beneath. "I was captured, held for a day, and then released. That's it."

"And how did that make you feel?" she probes.

"Trapped," I say, avoiding elaboration. I make no mention of the Valium I've been using to help me function, to help me forget. "Even now, I sometimes feel like I'm still in that room."

"It sounds like you're grappling with a complex form of trauma," she says softly, sensing there's more I'm not sharing. "And it's important to remember you're not alone, even if it feels that way."

"I usually prefer to be alone," I confess, adding a layer of context I've never ventured into before. "It's easier than worrying about who might let you down next. My father cheated on my mom multiple times. Growing up around that, you start to question the sincerity of every 'I love you' or 'I'm here for you.' You build these walls because you think they'll protect you, but all they really do is lock you in."

Dr. Diedra nods, absorbing my words. "It sounds like your father's actions have had a profound impact on your ability to trust. It's a defense mechanism, keeping people at arm's length."

"It's not just him, though," I continue, feeling a knot tighten in my chest. "I've had boyfriends who I never fully trusted, who I pushed away because letting them in felt like giving them permission to hurt me. So, I ended things before they had the chance."

"Your experience with your father created a template for you, one that told you not to trust, especially the men in your life," she observes. "But every new person isn't your father or your ex-boyfriends. You are allowed to rewrite that template."

"Is it that simple?" I ask, skeptical but intrigued. "Just write a new narrative for myself?"

"It's simple in theory but difficult in practice," Dr. Diedra admits. "It takes time to unlearn the protective behaviors we adopt. But it's the only way to open yourself up to healthier relationships and better understand yourself." I nod, contemplating her words. "Vulnerability is terrifying," she adds. "But it's also how we let someone truly see us. And perhaps that's what you need. A safe space to be seen and not judged."

I nod, taking in her wisdom even as I grapple with the fears that have long held me back. "Thank you, Dr. Diedra. This gives me a lot to think about."

"And remember," she adds as I stand to leave. "You don't have to go through this journey alone."

As I leave Dr. Diedra's office, her words cling to me like a second skin. Maybe it's not just the kidnapping stoking this wildfire of anxiety inside me. Maybe it's also this armor of mistrust I've spent years forging.

Rewriting that narrative feels both tempting and overwhelming. Can I really tear down these walls I've built to keep everyone out, including myself? And yet, as I mull it over, I realize that Kingsley might just be the one person I could consider lowering my guard for, the one person I could dare to trust.

Maybe, just maybe, that's a gamble worth taking.

17

KINGSLEY

"**S**tay back," I find myself saying, my protective instincts kicking in full force as we walk from Dr. Diedra's office to the café she picked out for breakfast.

It's a short walk, just a few hundred feet, but the distance might as well be miles, given the challenges it poses. No sooner do we hit the sidewalk than a group of teenage girls spot her, swarming like bees to honey. They're shouting, giggling, clamoring for selfies and autographs on everything from notebooks to their own arms.

I position myself subtly but effectively between Victoria and the excited fans, ensuring she has enough space while not being too intimidating. It's a fine line to walk, respecting her public persona while maintaining my role as her protector. But as I watch her interact with the young fans—her smile genuine but her eyes showing a hint of vulnerability—I know I'm right where I need to be. Right here, by her side, keeping her safe in every way I know how.

"Thanks, girls," she calls out, her smile genuine as they back away, their laughter echoing down the street.

Watching her, it's like she's straddling two different worlds—one of fame, the other of deeply personal challenges. She has this knack for showing the world a strong front while juggling a lot inside.

I guide her into a corner spot at the café, a cozy little nook away from prying eyes. "Two coffees, one black, the other with a dash of almond milk, and two servings of the sourdough avocado and scrambled eggs," I tell the waiter before he even gets a chance to hand us menus.

She looks up, eyebrows raised. "I was thinking pancakes."

"Protein's better for you," I say, and she nods, her gaze drifting back to the window and out to the ocean.

She's deep in thought, probably contemplating her session with Dr. Deidre.

The quiet between us isn't awkward, but it's loaded. I want to ask her how it went. I want to tell her I regret not staying with her last night, but I hesitate, fearing it might shatter this fragile thing we've got going.

Instead, I shoot for something else, something that has been on my mind since living with her for a few weeks now.

"Where are your friends, Victoria?"

She looks over at me, initially shocked at the question, then she settles back into her chair. "I had a group of friends since school, but ever since this fame thing started taking off, they acted all weird and bitchy. I just didn't have time to deal with all that."

"How long ago was that?"

"We lost touch about three years ago. But I have Rosie, and Isabella seems super cool, so..." her voice trails off as she fidgets her hands.

"Are you lonely?" The words cut through the air, blunt yet piercing.

My curiosity demands an answer, even if it's a question I hadn't planned on asking.

She lets out a sigh. "That's the funny thing about fame. The paradox of stardom is that you're known by millions of people, yet you can feel so alone when you're at the height of it all."

The waitress sets our meals down, but my eyes never stray from Victoria's. For a fleeting moment, I catch a glimpse of something in her gaze— a shadow of sadness lurking just behind those eyes.

Silence descends over us, and I glance over at her, captivated by the way the café's soft light dances through her auburn hair. It's like she's not just in my line of sight. She's in my veins. I'm not just hooked on her submission but on every laugh, smile, and complex layer of her that I've yet to uncover.

For the first time, it hits me...

... I don't just want to be her protector.

I've been a shield for people all my life—physically. There are walls I've built over the years, walls born from past wounds, and I've always been fine with them standing tall. But looking at her, I start to think maybe, just maybe, it's time for them to come down.

But for now, I just sip my coffee, giving her the space she seems to need.

As we step into her waterfront mansion laden with bags from the morning's retail therapy, she gives me a small smile. "I'm going to go sort through these in my room. See you in a bit?"

"Sure." I nod, watching as she retreats down the hallway, her auburn hair shimmering even in the muted light.

When my phone buzzes, the caller ID reads "Indy," and I feel a pang of guilt. I've been wrapped up in this assignment and haven't been keeping in contact with my sister like I should.

"Hey, sis," I answer, the guilt sneaking into my voice.

"Kingsley! Finally! How are you? We've missed hearing from you," she says, and I can almost see her smiling on the other end.

"I know, I know, and I'm sorry. I've been swamped with this new assignment. But that's no excuse. How's Texas. Is Mark treating you well?"

"We're doing great. Don't worry."

"I always worry, but I'm glad you're happy, Indy."

"How is it working for the Viki Slater?" she asks excitedly.

"It's not bad," I reply, keeping my choice of words short.

"What? You complained so much about Victoria being high-maintenance when you first got this assignment," Indy says, her voice warm but tinged with playful scrutiny. "But you sound... I don't know, lighter now. What gives?"

I chuckle, finding comfort in the familiar back-and-forth with my sister. "People can grow on you, you know?"

"Mm-hmm," she replies, drawing out the sound in a way that makes me know she's not buying it. "You've always been a tough nut to crack, but your tone's softer when you talk about her now. Spill."

I sigh, laughing a little. "Fine, I've had a change of heart, okay? She's been through a lot, and well, she's kind of impressive, actually. But don't read too much into it, sis."

"Too late, already reading into it," she teases. "You've never been one to wear your heart on your sleeve, but you're also a terrible liar when it comes to family. You like her, don't you?"

I pause, cautious. "I respect her, and I guess she's growing on me. But let's not jump the gun here. Work is work."

Indy goes quiet for a moment and then chuckles. "You've always known how to compartmentalize your life, big bro. But this time, it sounds like the lines are blurring a little. Just be careful, okay?"

"Yeah," I say softly, touched by her concern. "I will, don't worry. Thanks, Indy."

"No need to thank me. Just promise you'll call more often."

"I promise," I say, really meaning it. I miss my sister.

I hang up the phone, suddenly aware of the warmth flooding through me. Maybe it's because Indy's words have illuminated something I've been feeling but haven't wanted to admit. I glance toward the door that separates me from Victoria, and for the first time, it feels less like a boundary and more like a threshold I'm curious—but also a bit hesitant—to cross.

The smell of simmering red sauce wafts through the air, a scent so inviting it pulls me out of my room. I wander down the hallway and find Victoria in the kitchen, cooking away like she's in her own world. She's humming softly to herself, and for a moment, I just stand there, taking in the scene.

"Smells amazing." I finally announce my presence, not wanting to startle her.

She turns around, and her eyes meet mine. "Oh, hey. I figured we could use a home-cooked meal, you know?"

I can't help but smile at that. "You figured right. Need any help?"

She shakes her head, grinning. "I've got it under control, but you can keep me company."

We lapse into a comfortable silence, both occupied with our thoughts but content to be in the same space. I lean against the kitchen island, watching her stir the sauce, adding spices, and sampling for taste. It's a simple act, cooking, but it's intimate in a way, and I feel like I'm seeing another side of her.

She catches me staring and raises an eyebrow. "What? Do I have sauce on my face?"

I chuckle. "No, no. I was just thinking how different you look right now in the kitchen."

"Different good or different bad?" she inquires cautiously.

"Different good," I assure her. "Exceptionally good."

She serves me a plate of pasta, something I'd normally not eat, but the smell has me anticipating.

We have dinner, savoring each bite and sharing easy conversation, when suddenly she veers the topic toward my past.

"Do you want to share with me what happened in Somalia?" she asks tentatively.

The truth is, I do want to tell her. I'm just afraid she'll cast judgment like everyone else undoubtedly has. I'm not a hero. My medals aren't worth anything without my team, my friends.

She's still looking at me, and well, I cave.

"Just over a year ago, our regiment was sent in to negotiate a peace mission between the local villagers and the militia recruiting young boys to fight. We were a team of five, waiting for hours on end. The crew was tired, and I was spent, but I kept on the lookout while we took turns on point. It was my turn to rest, and I insisted on staying, but Roger wouldn't have it. He insisted I go back to the vehicles to refuel on water and food and to rest when I got there.

But when I did, all hell broke loose. The continuous rounds of bullets sounded in the distance. My team's voices echoed through the comms. One by one, they were taken down. And as I sprinted toward them, I knew in my heart what I was about to face.

But it was worse than I could have imagined. Two lay dead on the ground while militia pounded bullets from overhead. I took my spot and shot back while trying to pull my teammates to cover. I didn't know it at the time, but I'd been shot in the process."

"Is that the scar on your leg?" she inquires.

I nod. "I got it after a mission, a mission that went horribly wrong."

She gestures for me to continue.

"I was back at the truck when my team was fired upon. By the time I got back, it was too late. My team had killed most of the enemy, but it had cost them their own lives. I shot and killed the remaining enemy, and when I knew the threat was neutralized, I found my best friend, Carter, shot multiple times, bleeding out near me. I assessed his wounds, the blood pooling around us, and that's when I knew there was no hope. I stayed with him till the end."

Her eyes gloss over with tears, and I don't want her pity, but it does feel cathartic to share this with her.

"I brought every one of their bodies back, one by one, so they could have a proper military burial. Then, somehow, the state rewards me with a silver star." I shake my head.

Her hand lands on my arm. "You lost your friends in battle, but it's not your fault," she says. "You know that, don't you, Kingsley?"

I nod. "I know."

She pulls me into a hug, and my initial stiffness is soon replaced as I melt into her arms. For a moment, we just hold each other, a silent understanding passing between us. When we separate, I feel the atmosphere has shifted, grown lighter yet somehow more intimate. I place another delicious morsel of fettucine in my mouth and relish the home-cooked meal she made especially for me.

"You missed a bit," she points out, reaching up to wipe my mouth with her finger.

Just as she's about to clean her finger on a napkin, I grasp it and guide it back to my lips. Slowly, I lick the sauce off her finger, from the base all the way to the tip. Her eyes darken with intrigue. "Do you like it, Sir?" she asks, her voice tinged with the promise of play.

"Very much," I respond, and she gazes up at me through fluttering lashes. "Do you want to play, kitten?"

"Yes, Sir."

"I am going to wash every inch of you first, then reward you for pleasing me with a superb dinner," I say, tipping her head up and exposing the column of her neck.

"Yes, Kingsley," she says, and it's the first time she subbed out Sir for Kingsley. I like it. I like it so damn much I rake my teeth across her collarbone and nip along her jaw. She tips her head back and moans.

"Do you want a pussy full of my cock, kitten?"

"God, yes, Sir," she breathes out between kisses and bites.

18
VICTORIA

The steam fills the bathroom, mingling with the scents of vanilla and lavender as I step into the shower. The warm water feels like a gentle hug wrapping around me. He steps in behind me, our eyes locked in that glance we both understand. This shower is more than cleansing—an intimate act heightened by the raw confessions shared over dinner.

"Let me," he whispers, reaching for the shampoo bottle.

The air seems to thicken as his hands find my scalp. He massages the shampoo into my hair, and each circular motion sends a shiver down my spine. His touch is electrifying, turning this everyday act into something sensually charged.

I close my eyes, losing myself in the sensation. His fingers deftly navigate through every strand, lathering the shampoo while caressing my scalp in a massage. He gently tilts my head back to clear the shampoo from my hair and grabs the conditioner. His fingers don't just pass through as he massages it into my tresses. They linger, gently pulling at the tips. A thrill sweeps throughout me, electrifying my skin and quickening my pulse.

"Head back," he says as he circles the column of my neck with his hand, guiding me. His fingers gently squeeze my throat just as his fingers wrap around my stomach and dig into my folds.

I let out a moan.

"Such a good girl," he whispers against the shell of my ear as he sinks his fingers inside me harder and faster. "Kitten, can you handle coming twice for me?"

"Yes, Sir," I reply, full of need and already teetering on the edge.

He lowers his hand from my throat, and I feel it slide over my soapy bottom, caressing my curves. His thumb dips into my puckered entrance, and I let out a strangled moan.

Damn.

I need more.

Immediately, I press into his finger and feel his erect cock against me.

"Do you like me playing with your ass, kitten?" He presses his thumb in a little farther and, fuck me. My eyes nearly roll back into my head as I push back on him. He exhales sharply. "Fuck, you're a good girl. Come for me, baby."

With his fingers deep inside my pussy, he slides a full soapy thumb inside my ass, and I explode at the feeling, my knees weakening.

"Stay upright. I'm only halfway done with you." His fingers escape both entrances, and I'm barely standing when I feel a click.

"Back against the wall," he says and firmly pushes me against it.

The cold tiles send a blistering contrast against the heat of my skin, and he swallows my gasp with a heady kiss. His arousal is unmistakable, and I need him inside me. I reach out to touch him.

He shakes his head and clicks his tongue. "Impatient, kitten?"

I glance down to find he has removed the shower head, positioning it level with my clit. He clicks on the water, and I jump at the sensation as it hits my nub. He smiles darkly and adjusts the water flow, cycling through jet and rain settings, switching from back to front, edging closer, and moving away. He drops to his knees and kisses the insides of my thighs, then lavishes me with his tongue as the head stays on my clit. My legs shake as an orgasm builds quickly.

"Kingsley!" I scream as I unravel, untamed and uninhibited, gripping his shoulders for support.

"I could be undone by your moans and the taste of you," he says, his eyes so dark, so filled with an insatiable craving.

"I need to be inside you now," he declares. And honestly, I don't know if I can handle anymore, but with that intense gaze piercing through me, I know I'm all his.

"Wait here." He steps out of the shower, and when he returns, his hard cock is sheathed.

I can barely reach for a towel as I shut off the water, my anticipation building. But before I can wrap it around myself, he takes a step closer, eliminating any space between us. His hands gently rest on my waist, pulling me toward him. His eyes search mine for a brief second as if asking for silent permission.

Finding it, his lips meet mine in a soft, lingering kiss. My breath catches as he deepens it, his mouth moving in perfect harmony with mine. It feels as if every nerve ending is awake, magnifying this intimate touch.

Suddenly, he lifts me slightly, my back pressing against the tiled wall of the shower. The cool surface contrasts sharply with the heat radiating from our bodies. His mouth leaves mine to trail kisses down my neck, each one sending a bolt of electricity through me. His hands are everywhere, tracing the contours of my body as if he's trying to memorize them.

His lips find mine again, and this time, the kiss is urgent and passionate. This feels so intimate, like so much more than our original agreement.

I wrap my arms around him, pulling him closer, needing to feel as much of him as I can.

Then he sinks inside me, and I grip onto him tightly. It's fast yet sensual, a rush of sensation that consumes us both. We reach our climax almost simultaneously after just a few minutes.

When he finally breaks the kiss, he keeps his forehead pressed against mine. Our breaths sync as he meets my gaze, both of us suddenly aware of the gravity of what just unfolded between us.

19

KINGSLEY

When I woke up, she was already out of bed and changed into her active wear. It's a rare sight. Maybe it's the afterglow of last night, or maybe she's warming up to the idea of morning runs, but I'm so damn proud she's doing this for herself.

So, we run until she can't run anymore.

"You slept with me last night," she says, her voice carrying a note of curiosity when I offer her a bottle of water.

"You caught that, huh?" I take a long swig from a bottle of Evian in the kitchen.

"I liked it," she admits, her words catching me off guard in the best possible way.

"I did too," I confess, reminiscing about the feel of her soft breaths slowing as she drifted off in my arms.

She perches on a kitchen stool, her ocean-blue eyes locking onto mine as if searching for something buried deep within me. "What is it?" I ask, my voice betraying a hint of vulnerability.

"You gave me three orgasms in the shower, not two," she says, her words evoking a laugh from me.

I hadn't expected that, but it's true—I had only promised two.

"See what you do to me?" I tease. "I turn into an insatiable beast around you, Victoria."

She licks her lips, speckled with water droplets while contemplating her next words. "Are you like this with all your submissives?" Her voice wavers slightly, revealing her nervousness.

I step forward, my palms pressing against the table, an edge to my voice. "Are you seriously asking me that? Do you think you're just like the rest of them?"

She averts her eyes, suddenly self-conscious. "I don't know, I guess so."

"Victoria," I declare, locking eyes with her, "You're in a league of your own, far more than just a submissive in my life." And as I say it, I realize I'm also admitting it to myself for the first time.

Her eyes lift, meeting mine. "And you're more than my Dom, Kingsley."

The morning unfolds in a cozy manner as we share the workspace, each engrossed in our tasks. Despite our separate responsibilities, we find comfort in working side by side. In those moments between emails, her subtle glances in my direction feel like pure bliss.

When I drop her off at her session with Dr. Diedra, and she insists I take the hour for myself. So I find myself wandering the streets, idly looking in shop windows, when a voice I know too well catches me off guard.

"Kingsley, is that you?"

I turn, and it feels like someone just drove a knife into my gut. "Jackie."

She grins, throwing her arms around me. I can't reciprocate. My arms hang limply at my sides as memories crash over me like violent waves—her husband Carter's lifeless body in my arms, the stench of blood and gunpowder in Somalia.

She eventually pulls away, studying my face. I manage a forced smile, barely holding myself together. "How are you?" I choke out, even though it's a question that neither of us wants to answer.

She shrugs. It's been just over a year since that fateful day, and my eyes shift to the stroller she's pushing. Her husband never met his unborn child. It's like another knife twists, but right into my heart this time.

"I'm surviving," she says, her voice tinged with the kind of tired you can't sleep off. "Remy and me, we're surviving."

"I'm sorry I haven't been in touch," I mumble, my eyes unable to meet hers.

"You've done more than enough," she says, a tear escaping her eye. "You don't have to keep sending us money."

My hand shoots up, cutting her off. "I promised Carter I'd look after you both. It's the least I can do."

Her eyes search mine, seeing the torment probably mirrored in her own. She touches my face lightly, her fingers tracing the stress lines etched into my skin. "It's not your fault, Kingsley."

I clench my fists, my jaw ticking in rhythm with my racing heart. "Stop saying that."

"I will when you start believing it," she whispers, her

hand still on my face, forcing me to confront a reality I've been running from.

Just as I'm about to reply, my phone buzzes in my pocket. It's a text from Victoria telling me her counseling session is over. But another twist unravels before I can even contemplate the strange twist of fate that brought Jackie and me together again.

"Kingsley, there you are!" Victoria's voice calls out from down the street. As she approaches, I can't help but notice a flicker of jealousy cross her eyes when she sees me standing close to Jackie. It's a look I've never seen on her before, and oddly enough, I find it comforting.

"Victoria," I breathe out her name like a sigh of relief. "There's someone I want you to meet."

Jackie turns toward Victoria, and her eyes widen in recognition. "Oh my God, you're Viki Slate! I love your work!"

Victoria's eyes shift from jealousy to pleasant surprise. "Thank you, that means a lot to me. And you are?"

"This is Jackie," I say, feeling like I'm standing on a fault line between two seismic plates—my past and my present. "Jackie, meet Victoria. She's the reason I've been in Montauk. I'm her bodyguard."

Victoria extends her hand gracefully, but I see her eyes flick back to mine, still trying to read the unreadable. "It's nice to meet you, Jackie."

"Likewise," Jackie replies, shaking Victoria's hand.

The tension is still there, a taut string vibrating with unspoken words and unacknowledged feelings. But seeing the two of them together, I feel like I'm at a crossroads, and for the first time in years, either path seems bearable.

Victoria's eyes still probe. "So, how do you two really know each other?"

I glance at Jackie before turning back to Victoria. "I served with her husband, Carter."

The atmosphere shifts. Even the air feels heavier. Victoria's eyes widen, understanding the unspoken implications.

Jackie picks up where I left off. "Carter didn't make it back. But Kingsley here has been nothing short of a guardian angel since then." Her eyes meet mine, filled with a gratitude that makes my chest tighten. "He's made sure Remy and I are okay, even from a distance. I can never thank him enough."

Victoria's eyes turn soft, the jealousy replaced by something warmer that looks a lot like admiration. I can't help but feel awkward, undeserving of the praise. My eyes lower. It's all I can do to keep myself composed.

"I'm so sorry," Victoria says.

"Thank you," Jackie replies. "What are you two doing in Montauk? Do you have a concert I don't know about?" Jackie shifts the tone.

"No." She smiles. "Just taking some time off since..." Her voice hangs in the air as she chooses her next words carefully, "... since the Asian tour."

Jackie realizes, offering, "I'm sorry. I read about what happened to you there."

Both women smile. "It must be comforting to know you have a trained killer by your side now."

Victoria lets out a nervous laugh. "It is indeed."

I stare at the beautiful woman by my side as Jackie's words hang in the air. When our eyes lock, it's like striking a match—sudden and electrifying. My breath catches, and I notice her own breathing quicken. For that moment, everything else fades away, and it's just us. The world seems to shrink, Victoria my sole focus.

Jackie clears her throat, and I shift my attention,

noticing a wry smile touching her lips as if she's read the silent conversation happening in our stares.

"Well, I should get going," she says, gracefully withdrawing from the magnetic field Victoria and I have unknowingly created.

"Goodbye, Jackie," Victoria says, her voice slightly breathless. She then leans down toward the stroller. "And goodbye to you too, little Remy."

As Jackie wheels Remy away, I can't help but follow them with my eyes for a moment. Then I refocus on Victoria, whose gaze hasn't left me. She's standing closer now and pulls her hand, taking it in mine.

In her eyes, I see something that makes the heaviness of my past recede, even if just for a moment.

"How was your session?" I ask.

"Let's talk about that later." Victoria looks up at me. "There's something special I want to show you," she says, her voice tinged with excitement.

Intrigued, I find myself easily drawn into her gravitational pull as she takes the lead. We wander through Montauk's less-frequented streets, seemingly distancing ourselves from the hustle and bustle with every step. After a considerable walk, my curiosity finally gets the better of me.

"So, where exactly are you taking me?" I ask, a note of anticipation infiltrating my voice.

She turns her head slightly, giving me an enigmatic smile. "The question is, do you trust me enough to find out?"

Her inquiry takes me by surprise and makes me pause. Trust is a currency I'm usually very careful with, not willing to spend indiscriminately. But as our eyes lock, something inside me shifts. A startling realization surfaces—I do trust her. "Yes," I find myself saying, almost in disbelief at my own uncharacteristic openness. "Yes, I trust you."

Grinning broadly now, she guides me onto a hidden path that branches off the road. A canopy of leaves from towering trees envelops us as if nature itself is providing a sanctuary from the world's prying eyes. As we wind our way through this tucked-away trail, I instinctively reach out, taking her hand in mine.

"I have to admit, surprises are generally not on my list of favorite things. Given my line of work, they usually mean something's gone very wrong," I offer, though my tone betrays that my grumbling isn't completely serious.

Her laughter fills the air. "Oh, lighten up, Kingsley. Sometimes life needs a little unpredictability."

We reach the end of the tree-lined path, and Victoria suddenly turns to me, her eyes brimming with emotion. Without a word, she throws her arms around my neck and pulls me close. In that quiet, secluded space, she kisses me. The world falls away as her lips meet mine—passionate, urgent, and profoundly meaningful. When she finally pulls back, her eyes search mine. "You're a good man, Kingsley."

I'm left almost breathless, feeling like I've been given something I didn't know I was missing. It's like a reset button got hit, clearing away some of the self-doubt and guilt that's been hanging over me for ages. I'm falling head first, and I'm in unchartered territory, but I'm too fucking far gone to stay away.

The warmth of her smile reaches all the way to her eyes, making them shine even brighter. She pivots and takes my hand, enthusiastically pulling me. And then the forest opens up before us, and we emerge onto a secluded beach. Fine golden sand sprawls out, surrounded by boulders and the Atlantic waves. It's as if we've stumbled into a secret world, untouched and unspoiled. Hidden and so beautiful.

"I used to escape here during family vacations," she admits softly, her eyes drifting across the sand and water. "My parents would argue a lot, especially about my dad's... indiscretions. This place was my refuge from all that chaos."

In Sardinia, it was obvious that her parents' marriage was riddled with infidelities. Her father brazenly flirted with multiple women at the engagement party. But now, as she shares this with me, it's like she's peeling back a layer, allowing me a glimpse into her vulnerabilities. We're opening up, showing each other our scars. I grasp her hand a bit tighter, pulling her away from those haunting memories back to the present moment, from the complicated web of family issues to the simplicity of us, right here, right now.

"Thank you for trusting me with this." My eyes meet hers as I tuck a strand of windswept hair behind her ear.

"You're welcome, Kingsley," she replies, her fingers tightening around mine.

I draw her closer, and she slips comfortably under my arm.

20
VICTORIA

We're walking back from the beach, and a sense of lightness fills the air between Kingsley and me, talking and laughing like we've known each other for months, not a mere amount of weeks. I feel like I can share anything with this man.

It's too quick, right? It's too quick to fall in love with someone so soon.

But as soon as we step into the shopping area, screams rip through the atmosphere, shattering our bubble of contentment. "Madman!" "Knife!" Words fly, sharp and panicked, colliding into each other in the chaos. My heart kicks into high gear.

Every instinct screams at me to run. He grabs my hand, pushing our way through the crowd, and my eyes catch a terrifying scene.

A man, deranged and wielding a knife, staggers dangerously. A woman is on the ground nearby, gripping her injured leg but thankfully still conscious. My heart lurches into my throat.

Kingsley becomes a different person in that instant. His

body tightens, his eyes lock onto the threat, and suddenly, he's not just Kingsley. He's a soldier, ready for action.

"Down! Get down now!" he barks at the crowd, his voice carrying an authority that compels obedience. "Behind that car! You two, inside that store, lock the door!"

He looks at me, his gaze intense and urgent. "Victoria, go hide behind that dumpster and stay down."

I hesitate, gripping his hand tighter. The words are there, ready to spill from my lips. "Don't go, stay with me." Fear grips me at the thought of losing him.

"Victoria," he repeats, more firmly this time, breaking into my paralysis. "You need to hide. *Now.*"

I see the urgency in his eyes but also the faintest trace of fear—not for himself, but for me. Reluctantly, I let go of his hand and retreat behind the dumpster he indicated, my heart pounding so loudly it drowns out the chaos around me.

As he runs off, my eyes follow him, watching as he rushes toward the danger with a blend of skill and daring that leaves no doubt about his abilities.

Huddled behind the dumpster, I risk a peek to keep Kingsley in my view. He's rapidly closing in on the man with the knife, his movements both deliberate and deadly in their intent. Just as I catch my breath, the man lunges at Kingsley, knife aimed at his chest. Kingsley dodges it with a nimbleness that belies his size, a razor-thin margin separating him from the blade.

I let out a loud shriek, fear clouding my senses.

In a fluid motion, Kingsley counters, striking the man hard enough to jolt the weapon from his grip. It clatters to the ground, rendered useless. His fist connects with the man's jaw, and I hear a distinct crack from where I stand. The man crumbles to the ground, knocked out cold.

Police sirens scream in the distance, steadily getting louder. My heart pounds wildly, still coursing with adrenaline, but it's the kind that's starting to mix with relief and awe.

Kingsley's eyes dart around until they lock onto me, still tucked away in my hiding spot. His face, stern just moments before, softens in a way that makes my stomach flip.

He comes to me, his pace quick but measured, and when he reaches me, he wraps me in an embrace that feels like home, like safety. "Are you okay?" he asks, his voice heavy with emotion. He caresses my cheeks and continues, "I'm sorry I left you, but I had—"

"Kingsley, I'm fine." I nod, cutting him off, struggling to put my swirling emotions into words. The feelings overwhelming me are too complex, too new, but they all point to one irrefutable truth.

I don't just care about this man.

As we pull apart, the blaring sirens finally come to a stop, replaced by the chatter and footsteps of police officers securing the scene. Red and blue lights splash across the walls and pavement, signaling both crisis and control. The crowd begins to regather, their expressions transitioning from fear to relief and then to awe.

"There he is! The guy who took down the knifeman," someone shouts, pointing in our direction.

"He's a hero," another voice chimes in.

Kingsley's body tenses in the circle of my arms, uncomfortable under the weight of that word that evokes his past.

His eyes meet mine briefly as if seeking refuge before darting away. He's not one for the limelight, but isn't that a true hero? His actions weren't motivated by a desire for recognition. He acted because it was the right thing to do.

"Put your glasses on," he directs, putting me first and trying to shield me from any unwanted attention.

Before we can slip away, a police officer approaches us, his eyes focused on Kingsley. "Sir, we'll need to take your statement for the incident report."

As the police officer moves closer, intent on pulling Kingsley away for a debrief, Kingsley's eyes lock onto mine.

"I'm not leaving you again," he declares firmly, his gaze never wavering from mine. "She's coming with me."

The officer's eyes widen briefly before he gives a resigned nod. It's as if he grasps that whatever just happened between us has bound us together, a connection too potent for protocol or procedures to sever.

But he doesn't realize that we were bound long before this moment.

It's way past midnight when we finally exit the police station and head home. I find myself nestled in Kingsley's bed, his arm resting reassuringly over me as he drifts to sleep.

I listened intently as Kingsley gave his precise, methodical statement. By the end of it, the officers, who had pulled up his file, were practically huddled around him like groupies at a rock concert.

They'd already asked me for autographs for their wives —but Kingsley is the one who truly captivated their attention. It's his no-nonsense demeanor that people can't help but respect.

His kind heart, once you peel back the layers, and his belief in me draws me toward him in ways I hadn't anticipated. He might be a fortress of steel on the outside, but inside, he possesses an endless capacity for kindness and protectiveness. And it's disarming, unsettling in the best possible way.

It's not what I expected from him—not by a long shot—and it's thrown me into an emotional tailspin. One where I'm free-falling without a parachute, and I am pretty certain he may feel the same by every look, caress, and cuddle.

My eyes close, and I'm on the cusp of sleep when the haunting image of the man with the knife flashes before me. It triggers a torrent of memories, specifically of the knife my abductor once held. My heart skyrockets, pounding in my chest like a trapped bird. I try to shove the memory aside, but it digs in, worsening by the second.

A cold sweat breaks out across my skin, and panic constricts my throat. Slipping out of bed as quietly as possible, I dart from Kingsley's room to my own. Frantically, I dig through my bag for the small vial of Valium I packed, hoping to douse the rising panic.

Dr. Deirdra's words echo in my mind—panic surfing, she calls it. Riding out the wave of anxiety through focused breathing. But my breathing just makes me feel like I'm hyperventilating.

"Dammit!" I shout, frustrated with myself, and bolt into the bathroom, locking the door behind me.

I swipe the lid off, and it bobbles on the cold tiles. I'm clutching that tiny pill in my hand, teetering on the edge of taking it, just to make this unrelenting fear subside, when I hear a pounding on the door.

"Victoria, are you in there?" Kingsley's voice penetrates the fog of my panic.

I can't respond. My throat feels like it's lined with sandpaper.

"Victoria," he calls again, more urgently this time. And

before I can say anything, before I can pop that pill into my mouth, the door shatters inward.

Kingsley bursts in, his face lined with worry.

My tears start to flow as I curl up, cradling my legs to my chest. He sees the pill in my hand, and his eyes soften. Without a word, he lifts me from the cold tiles and pulls me tightly against his chest.

A strange calm starts to wash over me when I'm enveloped in his arms. "Shh... I'm here, baby," he whispers gently into my ear. "I need you to breathe with me. In for five seconds and then out."

I try to follow, but my breath is still coming out in choppy gasps. He stops, sets me down gently, and looks into my eyes. "You're having a panic attack. Follow my breathing, exactly. We'll get through this together. You can do this."

"I can't," I splutter out.

"In for one... two... three... four... five," he counts, his eyes never leaving mine, "... and then out..."

I try to mimic his breathing.

"You're safe," he emphasizes, giving my hand a reassuring squeeze as he exhales slowly. I find myself syncing my breathing with his, the rhythmic rise and fall of his chest helping to steady my own erratic breaths.

After a few minutes, the intense fear starts to ebb away, and I feel an urge to open up to Kingsley about what just happened to me. "Seeing that guy with a knife today brought back memories of when I was held captive."

"You're safe now," he reassures me, his voice gentle but firm. "You know that, don't you?"

I nod.

His fingers gently comb through my hair, and I feel a little more grounded with each stroke. "Have you talked about this with Dr. Diedra? Sometimes putting it into words can help," he suggests, his voice laced with concern.

"A little," I admit, biting my lip.

"Would you like to share more with me?" His sincere eyes compel me to open up. It's not just that I want to tell him—I need him to know. I need him to see the fragments, the parts of me I've hidden. Because somehow, I sense he'll still be here, holding me together, even after he knows all the broken pieces.

My throat is a desert, parched and aching.

The stench of decay fills the air, mingling with dust and sweat.

Am I dead?

I must be alive if I can smell the stench. I attempt to open my eyes, only to find a cloth bound tightly around my head, gripping me in darkness. A headache whirls, blinding and relentless, pounding its way into my very being. Nausea washes over me. I feel both ill and terrified.

My hands are trapped, tied behind me with a coarse rope that scratches my wrists. I twist and turn, but escape is impossible.

Panic seizes me. It's cold claws digging deep.

I've been taken.

Memories flood back all at once.

I was on stage, the crowd roaring, the lights of Tokyo's stadium all around me. Then, in my dressing room, the door flew open. A masked figure was there, something pressed to my mouth. Then darkness.

I can hear them, a distant rumble of voices like thunder on the horizon, twisted and unfamiliar. They're speaking Japanese, a language I recognize but don't understand.

Their tone chills me to the bone, filling me with an indefinable fear. Something about the malice in their voices tells me I am in grave danger.

With each panicked breath, my chest heaves, the terror inside me raw and all-consuming.

What do they want from me? Why did they take me? The questions claw at my mind but offer no answers, only more fear.

Tokyo. I was safe— adored. Top of the charts and top of the fucking world. Now I'm here, wherever here is, surrounded by darkness, my body trembling and tears stinging my eyes beneath the blindfold.

This could be it.

The end, when I'm only getting started.

The footsteps grow closer, and the voices become clearer. I can feel their intent. It's menacing, malicious, a dark energy that makes my skin crawl.

I want to scream, but all that escapes my lips is a whimper. I can't think. I can't move. I can only feel, and what I feel is terror.

"Please, let me go," I choke out, but my plea is met with laughter.

Cold, heartless laughter. They enjoy my fear. They revel in it.

The next thing I hear are footsteps drawing closer as one of my captors moves behind me. Then he says something to the other one.

My heart races, fear choking me as I sense that the worst is yet to come.

A rough hand grabs at my clothing, and the sound of fabric tearing buttons scattering across the hard floor echoes in the room. A chill rushes over my exposed skin, and a mixture of humiliation and terror washes over me.

He touches me again, and the stench of alcohol fills my nostrils, making me gag. His mouth is on my neck, his ragged breath brushing against my skin.

Oh my God. No.

"Get off me, you bastard!" I scream and writhe in my binds, but it only seems to spur him on. He becomes more aggressive, more impatient.

Hands fall to my waist and slide down my front.

No.

Please, someone.

Anyone?

I scream again, but no one is coming. I start to cry as he begins to assault me with his fingers.

Nausea claws at my throat, but I push it down. Then, that moment of clarity hits, and I realize I'm not dead yet. I can still fight.

With a surge of adrenaline, I manage to kick out of my bound ankle, my foot connecting with something solid. I hear him jerk back, followed by laughter from the others in the room. Then the air moves, pain explodes across my cheek as a hand strikes me, and I fall to the floor. My head hits the cold floor, and a shiver runs over me.

The room spins, and my mind races. I'm trapped, but I'm not defeated. I have to find a way out. I have to escape this nightmare.

The fear is stronger than ever, but now it's joined by anger, determination, and a will not to die today. Not at twenty-eight years old. Not with the world at my feet.

A phone rings just as I'm being pushed back upright. Its shrill tone, a dagger in my ears. A line of blood streaks my temple and runs down my cheek. I'm hurt, but it doesn't register.

I think I hear an American accent through the phone, then the shouting of my captors. Panic erupts. They are afraid, and their fear feeds my own, twisting it into something new. Hope? No, not hope. Not yet. Just a tiny spark of something less dark, less all-consuming.

Then, chaos. Shouting, scuffling, doors slamming, my senses try and keep up with it all. I'm adrift in a sea of confusion. What's happening?

My heart pounds in my ears, drowning out everything else. They're afraid. They've lost control. Could this be my chance?

I work at my bindings, my fingers clumsy and slow, but desperation drives me forward.

They've left.

The room is silent now, heavy with uncertainty.

I'm alone, bound but not broken.

"Victoria?" his voice snaps me back to the now.

I swallow down the sand in my throat. "After I was abducted, I woke up in an old, musty warehouse, my hands tied behind me. I was parched, sore, and bruised. My face felt swollen, as if I'd been hit, though I couldn't recall the moment it happened." Taking a deep breath to steady myself, I continue, "I heard foreign voices. There were two of them, taunting me." I close my eyes and inhale sharply. "One was behind me while the other slid his hand down my front and touched me inappropriately." My voice wavers, and tears fill my eyes as the memories resurface.

Kingsley's expression hardens, and I can see the muscles in his jaw clenching. "What? He touched you?"

Shaking my head, I confess, "I felt so ashamed."

"Victoria, this isn't your fault," he says emphatically. "Why didn't you include the assault in your police report?"

"I was too embarrassed," I admit. "Vincent and Julius were with me, and I feared what they might do if they found out."

He looks at me dumbfounded. "You were trying to protect them, even after what you'd been through? Jesus

Christ, do you know how incredibly strong you are, Victoria? You need to see that in yourself."

I can see something change in Kingsley's eyes—like a mixture of awe and deep respect, and maybe, just maybe, I think it too. He pulls me closer, and I tuck my head under his chin, feeling enveloped by his warmth.

The tension starts to drift away, replaced by a sense of safety and peace I've only ever felt in his arms.

"You need some rest," he says softly. "Sleep, beautiful." My eyes grow heavy, but before they completely shut, I feel his hand gently stroking my hair, and he pulls me close.

"I'm proud of you, Victoria. You're stronger than you give yourself credit for," he says, his voice low but filled with emotion.

I let out a sleepy sigh, my guard down, my mind foggy with the onset of sleep. "Don't leave me, Kingsley..." I murmur.

For a moment, there's silence. Then I feel his lips gently kiss my forehead. "Never," he

whispers, but I'm already slipping into sleep, comforted by the sound of his voice and the realization that my heart has found its home.

As I wake to the soft morning light filtering through the curtains, I'm momentarily disoriented. *Ah, my room.* The events of last night—the panic attack—flood back. Oddly, I don't feel as bad about it as I usually would. Rising from the bed, the aroma of breakfast lures me toward the kitchen, and I'm ready to start a new day, especially with him.

There he is, Kingsley, standing at the stove, flipping pancakes. It's a domestic scene, so at odds with the trained soldier of yesterday, but it's also reassuring in its normalcy and couldn't be more perfect.

"Morning," he says, not taking his eyes off the skillet. "Hope you're hungry."

I hesitate, feeling the weight of last night's emotional upheaval between us. "Kingsley, about last night... thank you—"

He sets the spatula down and turns to look at me. "You don't have to thank me, Victoria. We all have our demons, our moments. What's important is how we face them and who we choose to face them with. You chose me, and I feel forever grateful for your trust."

The sincerity in his eyes disarms me, and he offers me a slight smile that weakens my knees.

"Thank you," I manage to say, my voice barely above a whisper.

He picks up the spatula again, flips a golden pancake onto a plate, and sets it in front of me. "Eat up. We've got a new day ahead of us."

Sitting at the kitchen island, I take another bite of the delicious pancake, feeling a warmth spread through me that has nothing to do with the food. My eyes drift over to Kingsley, who's meticulously cleaning the skillet.

"You know, Mr. Disciplined, I'm surprised to see you flipping pancakes. No kale smoothies and raw eggs?"

He chuckles, turning off the stove and coming over to join me at the kitchen counter. "Ah, you've caught me. I do usually keep it pretty strict, but I figured today called for something special."

"Special? Really?" I arch an eyebrow, genuinely intrigued.

He slides into the chair beside me, our knees lightly

touching. "Yeah. I've learned that sometimes you have to make exceptions for exceptional people."

His eyes meet mine, and the electricity between us is palpable. For a guy who's usually all steel and edges, Kingsley sure knows how to turn on the charm when he wants to. And right now, I'm definitely not immune.

"So, what's the plan?" I ask, soaking my pancake into the sticky maple syrup.

"We're commandeering a boat for the day." Kingsley grins, his eyes sparkling with a secret he's been eager to reveal.

My fork hits the table with a clang. "Wow, really? Where to?"

"A secluded cove. You'll see. You'll love it," he says with a sly wink, making my heart boom.

21

KINGSLEY

The boat cuts through the open water, wind rustling our hair and salt clinging to our skin. I navigate us into the hidden cove, drop the anchor, and watch her reaction. The place is otherworldly with azure water so clear it's like a window to the coral world below.

"This is surreal, Kingsley. I never knew places like this existed," she says, awe filling her voice." How did you find it?"

"I'll be honest, I looked up Trip Advisor and, after scouring page after page, saw someone recommend this cove."

She laughs, her eyes twinkling. "Trip Advisor?" Unbuttoning her shirt and slipping off her skirt, she reveals a polka-dot bikini that instantly ramps up the temperature. "Let's swim," she suggests, and honestly, I can't think of a better idea.

We spend the day swimming, snorkeling, sunbathing, and eating a delicious picnic lunch of fresh fruits and salad. And as we head back to the marina, our eyes lock, and she gently squeezes my hand. The simple touch sends a wave of emotion through me, and I understand I'm not just falling for her. I'm already head over heels in love. The realization both thrills and terrifies me because I'm too damn scared I'll lose her.

She catches me staring and grins. "This is the best day, Kingsley. Thank you for this."

The sun is setting as I dock the boat and secure it. "Feel like some lobster?" I ask Victoria, pointing to the many chalkboard menus of the restaurants dotted along the jetty.

"Absolutely." She grins.

After walking for a bit, we find a seafood place, this one more private and less prone to unexpected, unwelcome encounters. We're seated at a rustic table with a waterfront view, and within minutes, two steaming lobsters are placed before us.

"I'm telling you, cracking a lobster is an art form," Victoria says, picking up her seafood cracker with flair.

I smirk. "An art form? Really?"

"Absolutely," she insists. "Watch and learn, Kingsley." She makes quick work of a claw, expertly breaking it open to reveal the tender meat inside. Then she dips it into the melted butter and takes a bite, her eyes closing briefly in delight. "See? Simple," she says, opening her eyes to meet mine.

"I can't wait to see you make that face tonight," I say in a hushed voice only she can hear.

Tension floods the space. "I'm looking forward to it, Sir."

She blushes, and damn, it takes my resolve from bending her over this table here and now.

"All right, let me give this 'art form' a shot." I reach for my lobster, gripping the cracker a bit too forcefully. The claw slips from my grasp, skitters across the table, and almost launches into the sea.

Victoria bursts into laughter. "I see your technique needs a little refining," she says, still giggling.

"I'm more of a shoot-it-and-grill-it kind of guy," I defend, but I'm laughing too.

"You're telling me Mr. Special Forces can take down armed criminals but can't crack open a lobster?"

"The two skill sets don't usually overlap," I say, feigning a serious tone, which only makes her laugh harder.

Finally, I manage to break open a claw, albeit clumsily. I look up to find Victoria watching me, her eyes soft, her smile gentler now but no less radiant.

"See? You're getting the hang of it," she says.

"Yeah, but I've got a long way to go before I master this 'art form,' " I admit.

A man approaches, dressed too impeccably for a casual harbor-side joint, and he wears a smirk that irks me instantly. My instincts tighten, and when he locks eyes with Victoria, her face tenses for just a moment before molding into polite recognition.

"Victoria, long time no see," he purrs, leaning in to kiss her cheek.

"Nicholas," she responds, maintaining her composure. "What brings you here?"

"Just in the neighborhood. Mind if I join you?"

Victoria looks at me, a subtle plea in her eyes. "Actually, we were just—"

"Who's this?" Nicholas interrupts, nodding toward me but not extending a hand. I feel like rendering him uncon-scious with one deft move.

"This is Kingsley," Victoria says, her voice treading cautiously.

Nicholas turns his smirk my way. "Pleasure to meet you, Kingsley. So, how do you fit into the picture?"

"I'm the man sitting across from her, sharing a meal. Isn't that enough?" I counter, making no effort to hide my irritation.

Nicholas chuckles. "Oh, so you're the bodyguard but off-duty, I see."

My knuckles whiten, but I keep my voice level. "I'm not her bodyguard tonight, just a man enjoying dinner with a wonderful woman."

Victoria's eyes flit to mine, a mixture of surprise and appreciation in her gaze. Sensing the tension but misinterpreting its cause, Nicholas leans closer to Victoria. "So, Victoria, still stunning as always. Are we going to catch up or what?" His hand inches toward her, a move so possessive it sends my blood boiling.

She pushes her chair back and rises. "Actually, Nicholas, we have plans. Kingsley, shall we?"

I leave enough money on the table to cover the bill and head out, my arm sliding protectively around her. We walk in silence until we're well away from the restaurant, then she sighs.

"He was an ex... one I'd like to forget."

"Let me make myself clear. I don't share, and if another man gets that close to you again, he'll spend a long time regretting it, bruised and bloody," I say, locking eyes with her to make sure my message lands.

She looks up at me, her eyes searching my face, and in that moment, I realize that if jealousy can spark a fire this hot, then what's brewing between us is an inferno. And I'm more than ready to get burned.

$\sim$

Back at the beach house, the air between us is thick with unspoken desire and unsaid emotion. We step through the front door, and Victoria turns to me, her eyes searching mine. I close the gap between us, my fingers gently tipping her chin up.

"You're mine, Victoria," I murmur, my voice tinged with possessiveness.

"Prove it," she challenges softly.

With a sense of urgency, I kiss her deeply as I guide her toward the bedroom, her lips parting willingly beneath mine. Once we reach the room, I turn her so her back is against the wall.

"Stay still," I command, holding her gaze.

I undress her, my hands quickly unbuttoning her blouse with each deliberate movement. And when the fabric falls to the floor, she's left standing in her bikini top and skirt. I take a step back to admire her. "Mmm, you look incredible like that."

Without breaking eye contact, I kneel to unzip her skirt, letting it pool around her ankles. Now, she's only in her swimsuit, her eyes holding a blend of anticipation and trust.

I stand and step closer, my hands moving to unclasp her bikini top. It joins the rest of her clothes, and I lean in to kiss her neck, trailing kisses down to her collarbone, my touch light but sure. I feel her shiver under my lips, and it fuels my growing desire.

I lift her up suddenly, our eyes locking as I carry her to the bed, where I lay her down gently, my body hovering over hers and my hand sliding beneath her bikini bottoms.

"Now," I say softly, my voice tinged with awe. "Stay very still for me. I'm going to make you feel so damn good."

22
VICTORIA

True to his word, Kingsley made me feel so damn good.

Twice.

The room is quiet, but my thoughts are anything but. The clock on the nightstand tells me it's late—too late for what's on my mind, maybe. But sleep is a far-off dream right now.

He's not asleep, either. His hand is warm in mine, yet the connection feels incomplete. Like there's a bridge we haven't crossed, a threshold we're hesitating to step over. I want to talk about it, but every time I try to form the words, they dissolve into a pool of insecurities and doubts.

I gently pull my hand away as if the physical distance will give me the courage to breach the emotional gap between us. My heart pounds in my chest, and I finally find the words. I almost lose them again in the thick air, but they tumble out, soft and shaky. "When you say you're mine, do you mean that for now or... for the long term?"

I hold my breath. It's out there now, and all I can do is wait for him to answer.

His silence stretches on, each tick of the clock amplifying the uncertainty that fills the room. I wonder if I've pushed too hard, asked too much, as he finally takes a breath to speak. "I like you, Victoria, I really do," he says, his voice low, like he's picking each word with care. "But commitment..." He lets his voice trail off.

"Sure, I understand," I blurt out, but inside, my heart is plummeting. *Had I misread every touch, every shared look?*

He adds, "I'm just not the guy who can promise forever. I've got my own issues, my own scars. I'm a mess, and you deserve better than that."

I feel like I've been punched in the gut. If only he knew that his perceived flaws, his 'damage,' is part of why I'm drawn to him. But now, hearing him say this, I'm starting to question everything.

Is this just another way for him to push me away? Because he's scared? Or am I truly the one who's been seeing this all wrong?

The weight of his admission settles between us. I could push him for more, ask him to face his fears, confront his wounds. But deep down, I know that's a battle he needs to fight on his own.

His words hang heavy in the air, each one landing like a little weight on my heart. I feel the sting of disappointment and a swell of sadness. I thought we were on the same page, but now it's clear that we're reading entirely different stories.

"If you're too afraid to let someone in because of your past, then maybe we should stop whatever this is."

He seems like he wants to say something else, perhaps an explanation or another half-hearted assurance.

But what's the point?

"Thank you for being honest," I continue, pulling the

covers around me a little tighter as if they could shield me from my own feelings. "I think it's best if we give each other some space to figure things out."

His nod is almost imperceptible in the dim light, and neither of us makes a move to bridge the newfound gap between us. I turn my back to him, needing the physical space to cope with the emotional distance he's placed between us.

For the first time in what feels like forever, the room is filled with a chilly silence rather than the comforting stillness of moments ago.

Closing my eyes, my mind a torrent of emotion, I realize the paradox of our situation. By not wanting to lose me, he's pushed me away. And although we're still lying next to each other, it feels like we're miles apart.

I wonder if this is the moment when we start to become strangers again.

A sliver of morning light slices through the curtains, painting a golden line across the empty space beside me. The bed feels too big, too vacant, echoing the hollowness I felt last night.

For a moment, I wonder if it was all just a dream—a twisted reminder of things hoped for but not attained. But then I see his running shoes missing from the corner of the room and the note left on his pillow.

Out for a run. Didn't want to wake you. Back soon.

It's a simple message, maybe even considerate in its intention, but it only serves to underscore the distance between us. We used to run together, share those early morning miles as a time to connect before the world woke up. Now, he's out there alone, and I'm left here with nothing but my thoughts and an empty bed.

I sit up, wrapping my arms around my knees. Hurt as I am, I can't shake the feeling that we're at a crossroads, each waiting for the other to make a move to define what we are or could be.

The door creaks open, and he walks in, sweaty and out of breath. His eyes meet mine, and for a second, I see a flicker of something—regret, maybe, or understanding. But it's gone as quickly as it came, replaced by that familiar guardedness.

"Good run?" I ask, injecting a casualness into my voice that I don't feel.

"Yeah, it was okay," he replies, avoiding my eyes as he grabs a towel.

He heads for the shower, and I'm left alone once again, staring at the empty space beside me. I can't help but think that sometimes the biggest distances are not measured in miles but in missed opportunities and unspoken feelings.

The water starts to run in the bathroom, drowning out the heavy silence. I realize that the gap between us is widening with each passing moment, each unsaid word, and I need to guard my heart.

I get up and start preparing for the day. Showering in my own room, my thoughts oscillate between Kingsley and work.

I spend most of the day sorting through emails, reviewing the upcoming schedule, and listening to recordings my producer has sent me.

This is where I belong, immersed in work, not isolated in the Hamptons, away from it all.

I call up Lexy, and she answers after one ring. "Viki! How's it going over there?"

"It's okay," I say, picking a piece of lint off my sundress. "I miss the pace of New York."

She exhales loudly. "It misses you too. Do you know how many things I've had to reshuffle and reschedule?"

"I know. I appreciate it, but I'm feeling better." There's a slight hesitation in my voice, but I push it away. I am feeling better since I shared what happened to me with Kingsley. It doesn't matter that we would never work out. He helped me through something, and I'll be forever grateful.

"You are? That's great! So, are you coming back to New York today?"

I'm surprised by her suggestion. I guess I hadn't really thought about it until now.

" I guess so," I say, shrugging my shoulders. "I'm keen to get back to the studio."

"So, can I say you're going to the Pop Music Awards on Saturday night?"

"Shit, I completely forgot about that. Yes, I'll be there," I say, not wanting to disappoint my fans.

"Excellent. I'll have Marie come around with a selection of outfits and book in hair and makeup."

"Great," I respond, excited to get glammed up again.

"Oh, and you're seated next to Justin Cole..."

I roll my eyes. Lexy has always thought it ideal to match the country singer, Justin, and me together. He's easy on the eyes and very talented, but he's not what I need, not what I want deep in my bones.

"Can't wait," I respond sarcastically.

"Huh! See you soon!" she says and hangs up.

I close my laptop with a decisive snap and pack my things into my bag. It's time to go.

Stepping outside, I spot Kingsley looking serious, his

eyes finally meeting mine. He's on the phone, and by the looks of it, he's not thrilled. He ends the call quickly and strides over to me.

"That was Lexy. Why are we going back to New York when you have another session scheduled with Dr. Deidra tomorrow?" Annoyance seeps through his words.

"I need to get back. I have an awards show in two days, and I'm feeling better," I say, offering a casual shrug. His gaze—those seriously piercing eyes—lock onto mine. "I'll do the session with Dr. Deidra tomorrow via Zoom," I add, recognizing the importance of maintaining my mental health.

"I'm not happy about this," he mutters.

"Well, I'm not here to please you, Kingsley."

His jaw clenches, ticking visibly. "No, you're not."

"I will collect my things and escort you back to New York, Miss Slater. We will depart in thirty minutes."

And there it is—walls up, barriers fortified. The brief glimpse of pain in his eyes reflects my own. But I can't let myself care. If he doesn't want me, fine. It's time to guard my heart and put distance between us for both our sakes.

In reality, he needs to be out of my life. I can't handle having him there but not really there, not the way I need him to be. I need to talk to Lexy about finding a replacement. It's the only way forward.

23

KINGSLEY

I'm kicking myself.

I had a stunning woman, one who genuinely wanted me, and the feelings were mutual. All I had to do was take the leap to give in to what we both clearly wanted. But no, I did what I always do—push her away and put walls up, all in a misguided attempt to protect myself from potential pain. I sabotaged us before we even had a chance.

I'm my own worst enemy.

As the car halts at the New York City curb, the glaring city lights seem intrusive compared to the mellow ambiance of the Hamptons. Victoria exits, arms wrapped tightly around herself. A defensive posture against the world, perhaps, or against me.

"Your bags will be sent up, Miss Slater," I say, my voice laced with a formality that now serves as a fortress around whatever almost bloomed between us.

"Thank you, Kingsley," she responds, her voice equally devoid of warmth.

She strides away, and despite myself, my eyes follow

her. This distance makes me feel ill. But then, who initiated this distance? The irony is not lost on me.

The walk inside is a vacuum of silence filled with words that should be spoken but aren't.

"I'll leave you alone," I finally say, handing her the bags.

"Busy few days ahead," she replies softly, avoiding my eyes. "Thanks for everything, Kingsley. I really mean it."

Her words prompt me to look at her fully, and for a fleeting second, I think I glimpse regret.

"You're welcome," I say, but the words are void of any real substance.

She hesitates, studying my expression before speaking again. "I think it's time we go our separate ways, Kingsley."

The words hit me like a ton of bricks, sending an almost physical jolt through me. I close my eyes momentarily as if doing so could shield me from the impact. "Of course," I finally say, my voice tinged with a heaviness I can't hide.

Her face takes on a look of sadness, but she quickly masks it, straightening her posture. "You're free to leave as soon as Lexy finds an adequate replacement for you."

Having seen Lexy's choices in the past, I'm not thrilled by the prospect. "Let me find the replacement. Someone I know I can trust."

She shrugs, her shoulders moving up and down dismissively as if she's already mentally moved on from the conversation. "Fine, whatever," she says, signaling the end of a discussion that changes everything yet resolves nothing.

As she retreats into her bedroom, I find myself rooted to the spot, torn between conflicting emotions. She's pulling away, and the unbearable truth is that I don't know if I should—or even could—draw her back.

She's right to stay away from me.

Heading back to my studio, each step is a monument to regret. My past, the team I lost, and the emotional scars I bear serve as armor against what could be an extraordinary relationship with her. And what makes it all the more agonizing is that with Victoria, I've felt a sense of completeness that I've never felt before.

The reality is harsh. I've driven her away to protect myself, to guard against the chance of another devastating loss. Yet, as I open the door to my suite, a crushing realization sets in.

I'm leaving.

She fired me.

I drop my bag with a thud and opt to pour myself a whiskey instead of unpacking. It's not like me, but then again, I'm not exactly myself these days.

I scan through emails detailing the layout for the awards show. It's being held at Madison Square Garden, so I familiarize myself with the entry and exit points and the security company in charge. They're a good outfit. I've worked with them before.

Victoria will be sitting in the front row, and there's a designated area where I can stand, although it's a good thirty feet away. Not ideal, but it's not like she can invite me as her plus-one.

Satisfied with the logistics and security details, I close my laptop and pour another glass. This time, I keep pouring until the glass is brimming.

Anger surges through me, mostly at myself. How can I be so adept at handling other people's problems but inept at dealing with my own? Why can't I move past the debilitating guilt over losing my comrades?

I know, logically, it wasn't my fault. I was near the military vehicles, out of range, when the enemy opened fire. But the question haunts me. *Why them and not me?* I wouldn't have to wake up each day shrouded in this suffocating cloak of self-loathing if it had been me.

I down the whiskey in a single gulp, feeling the burn trail down my throat as I immediately reach for the bottle to pour another. The liquid sloshes into the glass, amber and inviting, promising a brief respite from the relentless thoughts that hound me. I drink it as if trying to drown my sorrows, hoping the numbness will eclipse the pain, the guilt, the loss that never seems to let me be.

But as the fog in my mind starts to thicken, pushing me toward the blissful oblivion, I think I'm craving, something else emerges. It's her.

Her smile, radiant and warm, like the midday sun.

Her eyes, piercing and intimate, each lingering glance over the weeks seeming to understand and heal some of the jagged fragments within me.

The way her body feels pressed against mine, the perfection in our imperfect matching, it's as if we were sculpted to fit together.

And then there's the way she submits to me, a giving that's so much more than just physical—it reaches in and touches parts of me I thought were long buried under layers of armor and scar tissue. When she's with me and gives herself to me, I feel an unexpected sense of completeness, as if the missing pieces have suddenly been restored. For those moments, the world is right, and I'm whole, if only briefly.

The more I drink, the more I want to forget, to lose myself in the numbing embrace of alcohol. My thoughts of her are both a tonic and a poison, filling me with longing even as they remind me of what I've jeopardized. So I keep drinking, keep pouring, driven by a need to erase it all, the keen awareness of what I've lost.

Eventually, my hand grows unsteady, the room starts to spin, and I'm enveloped in the foggy haze of intoxication. Feeling my resolve weaken, and my consciousness wane, I slump further into the chair, almost welcoming the oblivion that follows.

Tonight, I want to pass out.

I want to escape.

And as the darkness closes in, I give in, letting it swallow me whole.

24
VICTORIA

Toni and her assistant deftly finish my hair, turning my auburn locks into silky waves. Meanwhile, Phoebe perfects my lips, her concentration unwavering. Everything has to be impeccable.

Battling the looming sadness, I force my focus onto tonight.

But my gaze keeps wandering to the tall man in the reflection, the one I fired but can't seem to forget. It's complicated, to say the least. My heart keeps punishing me, and being around him is a constant reminder of what we can't have—commitment. He's just not capable of it.

"Okay, stop fussing," Toni says, swatting her assistant away. "She's perfect." Her approval brings a sense of relief, and as she circles around me with her comb, I can't help but wonder how this evening will unfold, especially with him standing there, so near yet so distant.

Toni begins the process of packing up her things, and the atmosphere in the room is a mix of anticipation and jitters as we prepare for the upcoming event. Just as if on cue, Lexy reenters the room, a wide grin on her face.

"Justin Cole," Lexy announces with undeniable excitement. "He's like a sculpture of pure gold!"

We all share a hearty laugh at her playful description, and it's true. Justin Cole is not just any ordinary guest. He holds the prestigious title of GQ Man of the Year.

I see Kingsley's reflection, every muscle coiled like he's on the edge of something. He remains stoic, his face a mask of professionalism. But the subtle shift in his stance tells me he's warring with himself. It's maddening and infuriating because all I want is for him to finally let go and yield to whatever emotions he's stubbornly pushing down.

Lexy, the eternal matchmaker, doesn't miss a beat. "Did I say they've seated you two together?" She winks as if it needed any clarification that she's hoping for more than just a professional connection.

"Oh, lucky you. Justin is back on the market after parting ways with Victoria's Secret model, Carolina Decker," Lexy continues, her eyes twinkling mischievously.

Toni joins in with a gleeful "Yay!"

I'm trying to match their enthusiasm, but I think it falls short. "Well, it should be an interesting evening."

I marvel at my reflection. I've turned into a goddess at the hands of these masterful artists surrounding me. I look down at my satin blue dress with a plunging neckline and an equally daring low-cut back. My sky-high, needle-thin stilettos are the finishing touch, elevating my petite stature to something less easily dismissed.

I decide, then and there, not to let my heartache ruin my evening. "You know what, this evening's gonna be fun, and who knows what will happen with Justin," I say, my tone more casual and relaxed. I know nothing is going to happen. I'm nowhere near interested in Justin, but I'm finding the words tumble out of my mouth loud enough for Kingsley to hear.

"Miss Slater, it's time to leave." Kingsley's abrupt interruption jolts me from my thoughts. His words are direct and assertive and cause my team to stop what they are doing and stare.

He looks angry.

Good.

"It's a real loss, Kingsley, your departure. Who else will dazzle us with such unmatched bedside manner?" Lexy says, her words dripping with sarcasm.

"He's leaving so soon? Damn, he's quite easy on the eyes. Maybe I should check if he's up for something casual," Toni muses aloud.

The moment Toni's words fill the room, something inside me clenches. She's talking about him—about Kingsley—as if he's just another guy, a potential fling. Like he's up for grabs. My expression tightens.

"No," I interject, sharper than I intend to. "He's not like that." My words slice through the room, cutting off any further speculation about Kingsley.

Lexy turns to look at me, her eyes a mixture of confusion and curiosity. She's clearly trying to read the meaning behind my sudden vehemence, perhaps even wondering if there is anything going on between us.

"Miss Slater, we must go now," Kingsley announces, his voice breaking through the awkward tension like a knife. His tone leaves no room for argument.

My heart pounds relentlessly in my chest. I've already walked the red carpet and listened to the host's hilarious introduction, and now it's my turn to step out and present on stage.

God, please, not now.

"Are you okay?" Justin's voice interrupts my mounting dread. He's backstage with me, eyeing me like I'm an oddity. All night, he has flirted shamelessly.

"I'm fine," I respond, offering him the well-practiced, camera-ready smile that's seen me through countless public events.

"You look ravishing," he observes, letting his eyes roam freely over my body, lingering noticeably on my chest.

"You already said that," I reply, grateful when a producer approaches him, offering a brief reprieve.

I use the moment to engage in measured breathing, reminding myself that I'm in control. My hand grazes the small bag I brought, knowing it contains a bottle of Valium from Lexy. I could easily pop a pill to numb the nerves. It's a quick fix, a temporary reprieve, but it won't solve anything. My stomach churns, threatening to revolt.

Kingsley's also backstage, but he feels like a distant island, separated from me by an ocean of anxiety. I can't go to him. I must handle this on my own. My eyes lock with his, and he gives me a firm, almost reassuring nod.

I mentally rehearse the simple steps. *Read the autocue, announce the winner, and then make my exit.* Simple, right? But then I overhear a producer telling Justin about the record-breaking audience numbers for tonight—close to twenty million—and my stomach ties itself into even tighter knots. The walls seem to close in around me.

"Superb timing, especially with my new album," Justin chimes in.

I shut my eyes, focusing on my breathing. *In for five counts, out for five counts.* For the first time, I let go of what others might think of me and focus inward. But my mind betrays me, dragging up the memories of my abduction—the parched throat, the bound hands. I force my eyes open to reset the scene.

"Miss Slate, you look pale. Can I get you some water?" The producer's voice pulls me back to reality. Both she and Justin are now focused on me.

"Yeah, yeah, you do, love," Justin agrees,

"I just need a moment," I manage, retreating to a quieter spot.

"You're on in three minutes," she calls after me.

Before Kingsley even speaks, his presence wraps around me, unmistakable and commanding. "Victoria, you can do this," he says, his tone a mix of stern encouragement and quiet concern.

I turn to face him, my eyes brimming with tears I won't shed. "Kingsley, please go," I say, each word tinged with a sorrow I can't disguise.

"Victoria." he pleads.

"Just go!" My voice surges louder this time, fueled by all the pent-up emotions since the Hamptons.

The pain on his face is impossible to miss—it's like I've physically struck him. His eyes, usually so composed, show a flicker of something raw, something wounded. But he gets it. He steps back, giving me the room I've asked for but clearly hate needing.

As he moves to the sidelines, it's like he's leaving me a piece of that hurt as a parting gift, a reminder that this is something I have to face myself. For better or worse, I've asked for this space, and now he's giving it to me, as much as it seems to sting us both. I need to move on on my own.

"Miss Slate, we're ready for you," the ever-cheerful

producer announces, gesturing for me to join Justin, who's already lurking in the wings. My heart leaps into my throat.

"Okay, breathe. You've got this," I coach myself, feeling my legs propel me forward as if on autopilot. The stage awaits, and before I can second-guess anything, my name reverberates through the air.

"Please welcome to the stage three-time Grammy winner, Justin Cole, and the latest 'it girl' with five number-one hits in the USA right now, Viki Slate!"

Hearing my accomplishments rattled off to a room full of industry bigwigs should be daunting, but somehow, it's grounding. I take it as a reminder that I belong here, that I've earned this. Gripping onto that confidence, I prepare to step into the spotlight.

The sound of applause drowns out the pounding of my heart as Justin takes my arm, holding it a bit too tightly for comfort, and we step onto the stage. The glare of the stage lights nearly blinds me, turning the audience into a faceless void. A surge of adrenaline kicks in, almost like a shot of electricity running through my veins.

I can do this, I silently tell myself, gripping onto those words as if they're a lifeline. With each step, the mantra repeats in my head, fighting back the fear and uncertainty that have been my unwelcome companions all evening.

I can do this.

I have to.

The autocue is my guide, offering its rehearsed lines. *"My beautiful companion, Viki, and I are here to announce the Grammy for Best Up-and-Coming Artist."* But then Justin veers off-script, leaning into the mic with a confident grin.

"With a stunner like Viki by my side, how could the future of music not look good?" he says, flashing a wink at me and the audience.

It's like someone pulled the rug out from under me. My heart sinks into my stomach, panic clawing its way up my throat. I feel dizzy, disoriented. The weight of the room, the lights, the audience all press in on me all at once. I'm on the edge of unraveling, acutely aware that this moment could either break me or be a turning point.

Kingsley's gaze from the sideline burns into me, heavy with concern and layered with a complex emotion I can't decipher. It's as if he's silently pleading for me to pull through but also ready to step in if I falter.

The pressure is unbearable.

I draw in a shaky breath, caught in a heart-wrenching decision. Give into my fears or face them head-on in front of millions. It's a pivotal choice, one that feels like it could define more than just this evening.

Summoning every ounce of courage I have, I lean into the mic. "Well, if good looks could win Grammys, Justin, you'd need a whole new house just for your awards," I reply, adding my own wink for good measure.

The audience bursts into laughter, breaking the tension, and for the first time all evening, I breathe. Really breathe. Justin smiles, clearly impressed by my quick recovery, and I can't help but return it.

As he grabs the envelope and dramatically announces, "And the Award for Best Up-and-Coming Artist goes to..." My pounding heart takes on a new rhythm. It's no longer a beat of fear but one of triumph.

In facing a choice that seemed monumental, I chose to battle my fears, and that feels like the biggest victory of all.

The rest of the evening whirls by in a haze. Friends, colleagues, other artists—everyone's talking, congratulating, filling the air with a palpable sense of excitement. And yet, even as the awards ceremony comes to a close and the anticipation of the afterparty builds, it's Kingsley's presence that keeps pulling at my attention.

He's been quietly by my side, navigating me through the crowd. His silence is a comfortable one, but it's his smile that speaks volumes to me. As he guides me into the afterparty, I catch him looking at me with a mix of admiration and something else—something deeper.

He may not say it, but his smile confirms that he appreciates the personal triumph I experienced tonight. But at that moment, it hits me. His smile, as warm as it is, will never be enough to fill the space between us. He can't give me the acknowledgment I crave from him and the emotional closeness.

The realization causes a mixture of sadness and resolve to wash over me. I push past him, breaking our unspoken connection. Tonight, I'll lose myself in my own sea of triumph, a space where I don't have to wonder about the what-ifs and could-have-beens with Kingsley. I'll celebrate my victories, big and small, and try to forget how bad my heart is breaking for just a few hours.

25

KINGSLEY

The moment she steps out onto that stage, conquering her fears, it's like watching a super-nova explode. She's not just radiant. She's blinding. And that cobalt blue dress? Damn, it's as if it was sewn from the very fabric of her courage. But here I am, stuck on the sidelines, trying to quell the fire that's been smoldering inside me since I first met her.

And then there's that guy—Justin-fucking-Cole. The way he sidles up to her, laying on the charm, it's like a punch to my gut. I can't help but imagine my fist meeting his smug face. The jealousy coursing through me is a toxic mix of envy and possessiveness, and it's eating me alive.

It's not just a clash of emotions. It's a full-blown war, a volatile blend of love, desire, and a stinging sense of inade-quacy. It feels like I'm caught in an emotional crossfire, my heart and head at odds, both vulnerable targets.

I could throw caution to the wind, shatter every rule I've ever made, and just tell her. Lay it all on the line. But as she laughs at something he says, my courage falters. *Does she even see me anymore?* As much as I want to be the one who lights up her world, I have to ask myself—do I even belong in it? Because she deserves the universe, and right now, I'm not sure if I'm a star in her sky or just a fleeting comet.

The sudden crash of a tray hitting the floor pulls me out of my internal battle. Everyone else seems to go on with their chatter, their laughter as if nothing's happened. A young waitress is on her knees, trying to clean up the mess, and it's like I see a mirror image of how I feel—out of place, forgotten. So, I kneel down beside her to help.

"You don't have to," she says, a young face framed by wisps of hair that have escaped her bun. I notice she's pretty, but it doesn't stir anything in me. Not when my thoughts are consumed by another.

"It's fine," I assure her as we continue picking up shattered glass and fallen appetizers.

"You shouldn't be—" she starts to say, but I cut her off.

"I'm no one special," I tell her, and in this setting, it feels truer than ever.

Her eyes scan me quickly, picking up on my lack of designer threads or the polished air of a celebrity. "Have you ever been to anything this fancy?" she asks.

I pause and look around the grand ballroom, really seeing it for the first time tonight rather than focusing on *her*. It's an opulent display of luxury. Crystal chandeliers cast a warm glow on everyone below, intricate flower arrangements that look like they've been crafted by artists rather than florists, and walls plastered with high-tech graphics that shift and change, creating an almost ethereal atmosphere. Even the band, on stage at the far end of the room, looks like they've been plucked from a list of who's who in the music world.

And yet, despite all the glitz and glam, it feels hollow. Because the one person who can fill this emptiness inside me is across the room, probably not even aware that I'm here, helping a waitress pick up broken pieces from the floor. A fitting metaphor for my life right now, broken pieces and all.

As we finish cleaning up, I place the last of the broken shards into a bin. The waitress smiles at me, her eyes lingering just a bit too long. "Thank you, really. Most people here wouldn't have given it a second thought."

"No problem. It's just the right thing to do," I reply, a bit awkward with the attention she's giving me.

I'm not used to this kind of interaction, especially not here, in a place where I already feel like a fish out of water.

She leans in closer, her voice dropping to almost a whisper. "Well, if you ever want to escape this crowd, just know you've got a friend in the service industry."

I chuckle nervously. "I'll keep that in mind," I say, already looking for a way to excuse myself. "Anyway, you should get back to your work. Don't want to get you into trouble."

"Right," she says, taking a step back, but not before giving me one more lingering look.

As I turn to meld back into the crowd, my eyes find her —Victoria. For just a second, our gazes lock. I see something flicker in her eyes, something that looks a lot like jealousy, but then, just as quickly, it's gone. She turns back to Justin, laughter and smiles exchanged as if I never existed.

The second Justin leans in to whisper something in Victoria's ear, I can tell she's uncomfortable. Her body tenses, her face hardening just slightly. She subtly tries to push him back, a small but clear signal that he's crossed a line. But, either too drunk or arrogant to notice, Justin doesn't back off.

I can't just stand here anymore. My feet are already carrying me toward them, each step heavier than the last, propelled by a mix of adrenaline and fury. I'm about halfway to their booth when he does it—breaks through her defenses and kisses her.

Something primal within me surges to the surface the moment his lips touch hers. No more overthinking, no more weighing pros and cons. There's only action, pure and instinctive. My feet move almost of their own accord, eating up the distance between us in a few large strides.

I reach the secluded booth just as Victoria starts to push him back. My hand firmly grips Justin's shoulder, and I yank him away from her with a force that's both physical and laced with every repressed emotion I've been holding back.

"What the hell do you think you're doing?" I practically growl, my voice low but vibrating with anger.

Justin stumbles back, surprised and now sobering quickly under my gaze. Victoria looks up at me, her eyes wide, but I see a flash of something there—relief? Gratitude?

"I think you've had enough for the night," I say, locking eyes with Justin but speaking loud enough for Victoria to hear. "Time for you to leave."

Justin mumbles something under his breath, his eyes darting from me to Victoria, then around, likely looking for his security. After a second, he seems to think better of whatever protest he was about to make. He turns and walks away, casting one last resentful glance over his shoulder, muttering a few inaudible words.

My heart's still racing, my fists still clenched, but as I turn to look at Victoria, I feel a different kind of tension flood in, filling the spaces where the rage used to be. There's a lot to be said, a lot to be explained. But no words follow.

She looks at me disappointed. "Take me home, Kingsley."

We step into the house, the tension almost palpable, charged with a mingling of anger and need. The door clicks shut behind us, locking away the outside world and all its complications.

Victoria's heels and purse are casually discarded, as though shedding the last remnants of our public selves.

"Why did you make such a scene tonight?" she asks, irritation coloring her voice as she turns to look at me.

"Because I can't stand seeing some guy put his hands all over you," I snap, my own voice tinged with possessiveness that I too damn tired of hiding.

"And what about you? With the waitress?" Her eyes flash, and I'm reminded that jealousy cuts both ways.

I close the gap between us, leaning in close. "Do you really think a waitress could hold my attention when you're in the room?" I question, my voice low.

Blue eyes stare up at me. "I need this," she finally says, breaking the silence, her voice tinged with a vulnerability I've rarely heard from her. "I need to feel good, to feel wanted. Can you give me that tonight? Consider it a parting gift."

Who am I to deny her when she's voicing the very thing I've been craving but too afraid to admit?

26

VICTORIA

With no more words, he cups my face and pulls me into a searing kiss, pouring all the unspoken feelings, tension, and need into a single kiss.

We're ravenous for one another, and my hand grips his hair, pulling him closer so he's almost suffocating me with his strong lips. I groan in his mouth, feeling my thong moisten as he flicks his tongue across my lower lip, raking his teeth across it.

"Turn around," he says, pulling back. His eyes are dark, like the poison I need. He unbuttons the loop at the back of my dress, and his fingers brush against my skin. The satin dress falls to the floor, and I'm left standing in stilettos and a thong.

He steps back and circles me in a way I've come to love. My heart pounds as he walks behind me. I feel his warmth and want him to remove his tux, but I also like it when he's in command, telling me what he wants me to do next. Making me his. Owning me.

His tongue swipes at the shell of my ear as his breath

tickles it. "Being apart from you is a pain worse than death." His hands slide down the front, finding their way underneath my thong and sliding a finger into my wet folds.

I let out a breathy moan. "I know, Sir."

He thrusts his finger in and drags the wet up to my clit. Then his finger enters my mouth, and I suck it from base to tip. He removes it, dragging it around to my backside, roughly ripping my thong in two, eliciting a gasp from me. He fills me from behind and in front, finger fucking me and giving me what he knows I need.

"Oh God," I moan out as his mouth tracks kisses across my neck and down the curve of my shoulders. A scatter of goose bumps rises across my arms as he quickly pulls an orgasm from me.

Kingsley tenderly lifts my chin as I try to regain my breath. "Are you on birth control?" His voice is tinged with desperation, a hunger to feel every part of me.

"Yes," I respond, my voice just above a whisper.

"Because I need to feel every inch of you," he says, his voice filled with a raw urgency as he sets his jacket aside. The words send a shiver down my spine, amplifying the electric charge that's been building between us.

"I want that too," I admit. "Can I undress you, Sir? Because I can't wait to feel you inside me," I ask, my voice tinged with an urgency that matches his.

"Yes," he says.

My hands unbutton his shirt, feeling the steady rise and fall of his chest underneath. The shirt slips from his shoulders, landing softly on the floor. The tie follows, quickly removed and tossed aside, all the while his dark eyes watching me.

He reaches behind his back, unholstering a gun he sets

deliberately on the kitchen counter, the metal making a distinct clinking sound.

I step back slightly to take him in. His shirtless form, golden muscles, his eyes full of hunger and need mirror my own. He moves closer, his hands finding my waist and pulling me against him. Our lips meet in another searing kiss that only he can manage, and it pulls a strong emotion from me, knowing that this will be our last time together. He notices the shift in my eyes but doesn't say anything.

The pain in his eyes is almost heart-wrenching, a raw vulnerability that he doesn't often show. He leans in closer as if the proximity could somehow ease the emotional weight between us.

We both momentarily lose ourselves in the here and now with another kiss. His hands wander to the small of my back, pressing me even closer, trying to merge us into one. Then he lifts me effortlessly, placing me on the edge of the kitchen counter. Immediately, I wrap my legs around him, drawing him closer.

"Why do I feel like dying inside," he whispers against my lips, his voice low and husky.

"You know why."

Kingsley locks eyes with me, his mouth opening as if to speak. Whatever he's about to say feels monumental, and for a heartbeat, the world pauses.

Just when he's about to speak, something outside catches my eye. Before I can even process it, the sound of shattering glass echoes through the room, and a scream escapes my lips.

Almost instantly, Kingsley's already reaching for the gun he set on the kitchen counter, his movements swift with intent. A shape launches from the garden bed, approaching the house.

In that instant, the atmosphere changes from one of desire to an immediate, piercing alarm. His hand remains steady on the gun, but the air now crackles with an urgent electricity. I snatch up my dress, scrambling to cover myself.

"Get down, Victoria!" he commands.

The moment I duck behind the kitchen cupboards, my mind races—what happened to security at the front gate?

Peeking out, I see an intruder dressed in black, a gun in his hand. "Get out of my way!" he shouts, his accent unfamiliar. A gunshot rings out, and I scream, hands clamped over my ears.

Frantic, my eyes dart to Kingsley's location. He's crouched behind the living room couch, just a few yards from the approaching intruder. My heart pounds so hard it feels like it might leap out of my chest.

In a fluid motion, Kingsley springs from his crouch, rolls over the couch, and tackles the intruder to the ground.

Oh God.

Kingsley wrestles for the gun, but the other man is strong. They twist and turn, knocking over a chair in the process. The gun skids across the floor, momentarily out of reach for both of them. Kingsley gains the upper hand with a quick jab to the intruder's midsection.

Seizing the opportunity, I run out of the space and toward the gun. I'm not thinking, adrenaline is pumping. I squeeze the trigger, the shot firing in the air, and both the intruder and Kingsley freeze, the immediate threat of the weapon halting any further action.

Kingsley lands a solid punch on the man's jaw before rising to his feet. "Hand me the gun, Victoria!" he shouts.

My hands tremble when I pass the weapon over to him, my grip surprisingly strong despite my shaking.

Kingsley takes the gun, his eyes never leaving the intruder.

"Who are you?" Kingsley demands, his tone unyielding. The intruder remains silent, his eyes flicking briefly to the shattered window before locking back onto Kingsley.

Before anyone can say another word, the sound of sirens grows louder by the second. I quickly slip over my dress, hiding my nakedness.

Kingsley narrows his eyes, sensing the intruder's hesitation. "You're not giving me many options," he says in a low, icy voice. In a swift, calculated move, he steps forward and strikes the intruder across the face with the butt of the gun. The man staggers, disoriented, but Kingsley keeps the gun trained on him.

"Now," Kingsley seethes. "Who sent you? The next time I ask, you will see a bullet fly between your eyes."

Panting, the intruder finally breaks his silence. "Agunda," he grunts out, wincing from the pain of the blow.

Kingsley's eyes meet mine, and I see a flicker of realization mirrored in his gaze. The name Agunda triggers a memory—weren't they the ones who pulled off a high-profile theft from a celebrity in Paris last year?

Kingsley's focus snaps back to the intruder. "Was it Agunda in Japan too?" His voice is sharp, pressing for information about my kidnapping.

The intruder hesitates, the sirens growing louder in the background while police cars screech to a halt outside. Kingsley presses the barrel of the gun between the man's eyes, letting it rest on his skin—a nonverbal ultimatum.

"Yes, yes, okay!" the intruder finally blurts out just when a shout comes from outside.

"Stop! Police."

Kingsley keeps the gun trained on the man but shifts his

gaze toward the window, aware that law enforcement has finally arrived.

"Put down your weapon." Police come from every angle, filling the space, weapons drawn.

Kingsley steps back and lowers his gun.

"He's my bodyguard. That's the man you want," I say, pointing to the bloodied man on my rug.

Officers swarm the intruder, hauling him to his feet and escorting him to a waiting squad car. Kingsley turns back to me, pulling me into a protective embrace, just as a new voice interrupts us.

"Detective Wallace, I'll be handling this case," the man says, displaying his badge.

"We need your statements right away. The sooner we get the details, the better," he continues, flipping open a notepad.

I lock eyes with Kingsley. God, I want to hold onto this moment with him, especially when it feels like he's on the verge of revealing something significant. But I can't ignore the gravity of what just happened. Reluctantly, we both nod.

We recount our experiences, describing the break-in, the confrontation, and the intruder's admission about Agunda's involvement. As I mention Agunda and their notorious activities, including last year's incident in Paris, the detective's eyebrows shoot up.

"That's unexpected," he mutters before continuing. "You should know that we arrested Mr. Agunda and the ring leaders in his organization just a few hours ago in a joint operation between the FBI and MI5. The intruder you encountered must have been acting on earlier instructions."

Kingsley and I share a look of both relief and concern.

Detective Wallace snaps his notepad shut, his eyes narrowing when he digests what we've told him. "Thank you both for your statements. With what you've given us, it looks like Agunda won't be seeing the light of day for a while."

A sense of relief floods over me, but it's tinged with the complexity of everything else going on, especially between Kingsley and me. Our eyes meet again, and I wonder what he's thinking, what he's feeling.

Detective Wallace heads toward the door, pausing before exiting. "You might want to put on a shirt," he says with a wry smile.

Kingsley grunts and rolls his eyes, and I can't help but smile, even under the circumstances.

After Detective Wallace leaves, the atmosphere in the room is heavy with both relief and the unspoken acknowledgment of what we've been through. Kingsley turns to me, his eyes searching mine as if to assure himself that I'm truly unharmed.

"Hey," he says softly, his voice tinged with both relief and concern. "It's over now. They've got him and his whole gang. You're safe."

As the weight of his words sinks in, a sense of profound relief washes over me. For the first time in what feels like forever, I allow myself to believe that I can put this terrifying chapter behind me.

I walk over to him and put my arms around him. He pulls me close, holding me tightly as though shielding me from the world's dangers. At that moment, I feel an overwhelming sense of gratitude and love for this man who has stood by me through it all.

Kingsley's eyes linger on me, a mix of relief and something deeper—something that's been haunting him long before tonight's incident. He takes a deep breath as if mustering the courage to dive into an internal battle he's been waging. "You know..." he starts hesitantly, "... tonight brought back memories... painful ones... of times when I couldn't protect the people I cared about."

I sense the gravity of his admission and grasp his hands, willing him to look at me. "Sometimes, terrible things happen that are beyond our control," I tell him.

"I know that here..." he points to his head, "... but feeling it here..." he moves his hand over his heart, "... that's a different story. I was so afraid of losing you, Victoria, that I pushed you away."

Our foreheads touch just barely, and my heart slams against my chest. Kingsley's eyes, a swirl of emotions, fix on mine. Then, like the eye of a storm finding its center, his gaze sharpens. "I want all my nexts to be with you, Victoria." He caresses my cheek tenderly as he continues, "I'm done running from my past. I want to face the future with you."

"Why?" I blubber out so emotionally I need to hear him say the words we've both pushed down for fear of being hurt.

"Because I'm so damn in love with you."

I sob out at his admission. "I'm in love with you too."

Immediately, he pulls me into a deep, soulful kiss, sealing a pact that's more powerful than any spoken vow. As we break apart, I see a glimmer of peace in his eyes I haven't seen before.

"Thank you," he whispers.

"For what?" I ask.

His dark eyes stare into my soul. "For reminding me that even warriors need to heal and that true strength lies in embracing vulnerability... with the ones who matter most."

EPILOGUE

Today, I laid down the final track for the album, and the sense of accomplishment is exhilarating.

I step into our house, still buzzing from the energy at the recording studio. The aroma of something delicious cooking fills the air as I drop my bag and kick off my shoes.

Kingsley sits at our kitchen table, lost in a sea of paperwork. He's traded his role as my bodyguard for a more personal mission—helping fellow ex-soldiers manage their PTSD. And the look of deep concentration he often wears after a challenging day at the center seems to have lightened a bit.

"Hey," I say, leaning in to plant a kiss on his cheek. "How was your day?"

He glances up, the typical hard lines around his eyes softening. "It was intense, but we made some progress. One of the guys started opening up today."

I beam at him, thrilled by the important work he's doing. "That's incredible, Kingsley. You're changing lives."

He wraps his arms around me and inhales deeply as

though he's treasuring the very scent of this moment. "The feeling's mutual," he says softly. "Your music is touching people, giving them something to relate to. We're both making waves in our own ways."

"I may have wrapped up my album today," I tell him.

"Then my kitten must be rewarded for all her efforts…"

I blush, leaning in to kiss him, only to be interrupted by my phone's the piercing ringtone.

Isabella's name lights up the screen, and I can't help but smile. We've grown close over the past few months, sharing regular dinners with her, her adorable son Fox, and my brother Julius. And naturally, they've all fallen for Kingsley just like I have.

"Hey, Bella," I say, my voice tinged with the happiness that Kingsley brings me. I press my lips to his briefly, savoring the moment before pulling away to focus on the call. "What's up, hun?"

"I'm engaged!" she shrieks down the line.

I spin on my heel and scream into the receiver. "What?"

"Your brother proposed. Just now."

My heart skips a beat, a surge of euphoria flooding through me as I hear her joyful screams.

"Now we have your wedding and Rosie's to plan!" I shriek with excitement.

A voice interrupts us, making me spin around.

There he is, Kingsley, down on one knee, his eyes shimmering with hope and love. "And ours… I hope." His piercing eyes lock onto mine, the weight of his words hanging in the air between us. "Victoria, marry me and make me the happiest goddamn man in the world."

I'm so stunned my phone slips from my grasp, forgotten on the floor. My hands fly to my mouth, a gasp escaping my lips when tears flood my eyes.

Dropping to my knees to meet him, I throw my arms around his neck, the words tumbling out of me like a waterfall of joy. "Yes, Kingsley! A million times, *yes!*"

His eyes—those dark, deep pools that I've lost myself in countless times—are filled with emotion he rarely shows. He slides the ring onto my finger. It's a perfect fit, like the life we're building together.

The moment his lips meet mine, everything else fades away. It's just us, wrapped in our own world, sealing a promise that's been in the making since the day we met. His arms tighten around me as if he's pulling me into his very soul, and I melt into him.

We break away, slightly breathless but smiling like fools.

A crackle comes over the phone that's on the floor beside me. "Oh... my... God... Victoria, are you engaged?"

The end...

...and their beginning.

WANT MORE?

Interested in a brother's best friend romance?

Devour the Elite Men of Manhattan, and start with Lourde and Barrett's sizzling romance in Forbidden Lust.

Available from all leading retailers or buy direct from Missy and save! www.authormissywalker.com

ALSO BY MISSY WALKER

ELITE MAFIA OF NEW YORK SERIES

Cruel Lust

Stolen Love

Finding Love

SLATER SIBLINGS SERIES

Hungry Heart

Chained Heart

Iron Heart

ELITE MEN OF MANHATTAN SERIES

Forbidden Lust*

Forbidden Love*

Lost Love

Missing Love

Guarded Love

Infinite Love

SMALL TOWN DESIRES SERIES

Trusting the Rockstar

Trusting the Ex

Trusting the Player

**Forbidden Lust/Love are a duet and to be read in order. All other books are stand alones.*

ACKNOWLEDGMENTS

I've always had a deep desire to write a bodyguard romance, and I'm absolutely thrilled that I took the plunge. In fact, I'm already feeling the itch to start working on another one.

A huge thanks to my Beta readers: Ella, Maria, Lauren, and Dr. Sas! I love and adore each of your comments and suggestions, and the little crew we've created while writing the Slater Siblings Series.

A massive shoutout to my incredible editors, Chantell and Nicki. Your support and expertise are indispensable to my craft.

To the fans:

Creating steamy escapes with Happy Ever Afters is my daily mission. We all lead hectic, busy lives, and we all want to be transported into a world where we can live vicariously through others.

I hope my characters provide you with the escape and 'me time' we all deserve. It is truly humbling to have so many readers out there enjoying my books. And it's because of you that I get to do what I love each and every day. For that, I am eternally grateful.

Till the next book...

Missy xxx

About the Author

Missy is an Australian author who writes kissing books with equal parts angst and steam. She loves writing stories about billionaires, playboys & forbidden romance – just to name a few.

When she's not writing, she's taking care of her two daughters and doting husband and conjuring up her next saucy plot.

Inspired by the acreage she lives on, Missy regularly distracts herself by visiting her orchard, baking naughty but delicious foods, and socialising with her girl squad.

Then there's her overweight cat—Charlie, dog—Benji, chickens, and bees if she needed another excuse to pass the time.

If you like Missy Walker's books, consider leaving a review and following her here:

tiktok.com/@authormissywalker
instagram.com/missywalkerauthor
facebook.com/AuthorMissyWalker
Private Reader Group -
https://www.facebook.com/groups/
missywalkersbookbabes